Catching up with his charge's group at last, the heir's chief bodyguard eyed the assault boats from the far end of the street. Perhaps these children could be persuaded to find more suitable entertainment. Though six Navy assault boats seemed a lot to discipline a baker's dozen of unruly adolescents. He hailed the assault boats.

"McModor here, from the Secretary's Guard," he sent. "Come to fetch the Sclerida boy?"

There was no response.

"I'm not reading anything off them," said his second. "No hull signals, nothing."

"This doesn't feel right." McModor hit the send key again. "Lieutenant McModor of the Secretary's Guard, hailing Naval assault boat, please respond."

The answer this time came from the boat's guns.

David Drake's
Crisis of Empire Series

An Honorable Defense, with Thomas T. Thomas
Cluster Command, with W.C. Dietz
The War Machine, with Roger MacBride Allen
Crown of Empire, by Chelsea Quinn Yarbro

CHELSEA
QUINN YARBRO

CROWN OF EMPIRE

Copyright © 1994 by Bill Fawcett & Associates

A Baen Books Original

Baen Publishing Enterprises
P.O. Box 1403
Riverdale, NY 10471

ISBN: 0-671-72208-5

Cover art by Paul Alexander

First printing, February 1994

Distributed by Paramount
1230 Avenue of the Americas
New York, NY 10020

Printed in the United States of America

Chapter 1

Tira Bouriere leaped upright in bed as her elderly cousin Helga burst in from her own small room of the suite, shouting, "He's dead! Your sainted father is *dead*, child!"

Behind Helga, the holovision the old woman had been watching still cast its faint light over the room. The royal suites on two of the four penthouse towers around the quadrangle had visual access to most of the High Secretary's palace. Other women her age might have spent their free time in gossip, but Helga considered her station — companion and chaperone to the High Secretary's eighteen-year-old daughter — put her above that. Instead, she spied on the goings and comings, the talk and the actions, of all those living in the sprawling warren of the palace, seat of government and home to the elite of the Pact which ruled four thousand worlds.

Tira pushed her way through the gauze that wrapped her bed like a cloud. "Helga, *what's* happened?" she asked. She'd heard the words, but there was no sense to them.

Helga flopped onto a loveseat, hyperventilating. Cousin by convenience, the connection was too diffuse to be recognized — except that the office of High Secretary drew to it relations the way honey draws flies. Even Helga's Bouriere surname came from her maternal line, and that three generations ago.

"Helga!" Tira repeated.

Helga stared at her from the loveseat. "Your sainted father," she repeated in a whisper. The utter despair in the old woman's eyes and voice penetrated to Tira's understanding where the words themselves had not.

2

"Oh, no. Not my father." For a moment hysteria threatened to overwhelm Tira's normal good sense. Then, as if a relay had switched in her brain, she became efficient, doing almost by rote the things she had been taught since she was a child. When she was young, the drills for this eventuality had been a game. She had enjoyed out-thinking the evil rebels who strove to endanger the High Secretary. It would have been comforting to make herself believe it was still a game. But this time she knew she would not be permitted to ask for time out.

She resisted her first impulse, to go to the window, knowing that could expose her to discovery and attack. She moved quickly to the inner wall of the reception room. Against the wall was a massive Neo-Empire Revivalist writing table, with thin, spiral legs atop traditional crocodile feet, all in gold. The writing surface was a vast expanse of malachite, edged in beveled gold work. Seating herself, Tira toggled two hidden levers in the table. The green surface lifted up and back, revealing Tira's internal security hologram station.

On the loveseat Cousin Helga was fanning herself with an infopak, heedless of the damage she might be inflicting on the contents of the tamper-sensitive device. She had unfastened the silver-net fichu around her neck and given it to one of the three servobots who tended to the needs of Tira's visitors.

At her desk, Tira was trying the fourth of twelve sets of codes that might show her what was happening in her father's apartments. Normally it didn't matter that his quarters were two towers away from her, accessible only by a maze of corridors. "It's wrong," she muttered, her attractive face marked by worry and the first real touches of fear. She tried another, yet higher, security code. Nothing. Again. More blankness.

After running through all dozen combinations she was forced to admit that there was a blackout on her father's apartments. With growing apprehension, she tried to reach her brother's suite, with the same results. Again she refrained from presenting herself at the window, turned and tilted one of the three vanity mirrors so that she could watch the outside in its depths.

"Oh, how distressing it all is," said Cousin Helga, at last putting the infopak down. "Just when I think I can bear to remember it — "

"Contain yourself, Cousin," Tira snapped. "Go begin emergency evacuation procedures. At once."

"Naturally. Sorry. I should have started immediately I reached here." The old lady stumbled to her feet. "You'll think I've gone foolish on you. And at such a time."

"Impossible, Cousin Helga," said Tira more kindly, abandoning her search. It wouldn't do to totally demoralize her sole ally of the moment.

Two alarms, one shrill and weepy, the other aggressive, went off at once.

Helga shrieked and bolted for the living room of the suite. From Helga's own room, which no one but she should have been able to enter from the corridor, stamped a squad of armed soldiers in brown uniforms, with Treasury collar flashes.

Tira rose to her feet, indignation warring with fear. As she did so, she pressed the toggle that summoned her own guards, waiting in the corridor. "What are you doing here?"

The man who seemed to be in charge remained motionless as the others fanned out to cover the room. "You must come with us," he said flatly, seemingly indifferent to her response.

Tira wanted to stomp hard on his foot and pound the heel of her hand into his nose. But there was something so disinterested, so lethal about the man, that she suspected he would not prove the easy victim her guard-instructors were.

"Now," said the man.

Tira remained frozen.

Suddenly, the tableau was interrupted when the door at the other end of the reception chamber burst open, and a young lieutenant appeared, a squad of twenty jostling in behind him.

The Treasury men did not wait for the new arrivals to get organized. Instantly the chamber was filled with deadly spangles as accelerated glass beads exploded into walls and malachite and flesh.

Tira, true to her own training, found herself crouched beneath her desk, totally helpless, as others battled to decide her fate. Totally helpless? Perhaps not. For her twelfth birthday her father had had installed a fabulously expensive fantasy simulator in her desk. It had been all the rage with her crowd for weeks. One stealthy hand reached up to the keypad set in the malachite.

From the various holographic panels and baffles there sprang forth a steady profusion of monsters. The first was a quite nasty basilisk, jagged spears flashing from his eyes. Then a trio of harpies, each with meat dripping from her talons. A streamlined snail with several leech-like heads undulated along the polished stone floor leaving a very believable trail of slime. A werejaguar, still human enough to be recognizable,

leaped and growled and spat, threatening everyone with daggered hands.

Not being idiots, the soldiers recognized holographic fantasy monsters when they saw them —
but not before drill-honed reflexes had spewed
beads in all the wrong places. The new arrivals, a
little more distant from the fantasy threat, took
their opportunity.

The sound crescendoed as the glass battered
everything in the room. A gorgeous authentic
snow-wood was chewed to sawdust by the cross-
fire. Many of Tira's other carefully collected
objets d'art were shattered and added their collapse to the cacophony.

Phantoms battled and thundered and rol-
licked as men fought and died real deaths.

Almost safe beneath her armored desk, Tira was
aghast at all the blood, steam rising from it as it
welled and gouted like lava out of fallen men.
Where it fell, bits of glass mixed with it, like a mon-
strous sparkling wine. She lay with debris pressing
against her cheek, and her hands were starting to
feel crusty where the blood was clotting around her
fingers. She didn't think any of it was her own.

"I've got to get out of here," she said to the air.
"I've got to."

As if mocking her plea, a gryphon capered by,
wings spread and talons extended, lion-legs and

haunches huge with muscles; its image was penetrated by a lieutenant of her guards, trying to reach her. An injured Treasury soldier was struggling to rise, lost traction on the gore beneath his feet and fell heavily, cutting his hands on the bits of broken glass as he struck the floor and dropped his weapon. The guard lieutenant set his pistol and fired.

"Demoiselle, we must leave *now!*" In the sudden silence of momentary victory, the lieutenant spoke with an urgency underlined by his grip on her arm. "Come. Hurry."

Only now aware that the battle was really over, Tira did as she was bid, absently dismissing with a flick of her hand the capering apparitions — who instantly ceased to obscure a scene of mundane carnage. Of the Treasury men, only two seemed likely to survive. One was whimpering steadily, his hands cupped over a foaming, sucking hole in his chest. The other was very pale, huddled in on himself.

"Martyrs of the Guard," whispered Tira, who had only seen incidents like this in entertainments. She put her hand to her throat and felt the speed of her pulse, fast and light. The smell began to overwhelm her senses. . . .

"Come on," urged Lieutenant Chaney — identified by his helmet and breast clips.

Tira focused on him. "Where?"

"Away from here," said Chaney. "They'll be back for you." He lowered his head. "Look. Demoiselle, you don't have to listen to anything I say. We both know that. But if you don't get out of here in pretty short order, you're going to be in trouble."

"Right," she said heavily. "Trouble." She shivered once, quite violently, then brought herself back under control. "Then let's go."

"All right, Demoiselle." He took her by the arm again. "So you won't stumble. You don't have grippers on your soles and I do."

"Very sensible," she said, glancing around the corpse-strewn room. Of Cousin Helga there was no sign. Tira decided she would have to ask later, when they were safe. At least she was not one of the ruined bodies on the floor.

The lieutenant led her to the main door, muttering to himself all the way. It took Tira several steps to realize he was talking to his AID. Almost all military had those personal communicating devices. No doubt he was relaying information to his superior. At the door, he leaned through cautiously, then pulled her along by the wrist. She jerked her hand away from him and he turned to glare at her.

She stared back. He might have just saved her

life but she was still the High Secretary's daughter. He nodded, took his hand off her and led the way between two shattered pier mirrors into a space that seemed much wider than it ought to be. "What — ?"

"Emergency hologram. It makes the exit look about three inches wide, doesn't it?" He chuckled. "Come on. There's . . . " He paused and stepped back between the mirrors.

Even though the secret exit was only a few steps from her suite Tira had had no idea it existed. It was that kind of palace. Through the hologram distortion, Tira could see what the lieutenant was doing: he had reached back to the nearest fallen Treasury soldier and was prying the dead hand from around the pistol. As he ducked back into the exit, he handed it to her. "Here, this is a Samtoepoe A7mark923, capable of semi or fully automatic fire with a clip capacity of 150 rounds. Don't use it unless you have to. Sometimes the A7mark923s jam. They cycle too fast."

"You took it —"

He did not permit her to finish. "I took it from someone who was prepared to use it on you. Remember that, if you start getting sentimental about the Treasury soldiers. They invaded. They don't deserve your concern." He waved her toward a protected dropshaft. "Military-only," he informed her, indicating the masking. "They're going to shut these down pretty quickly."

"You're right," said Tira, resolutely slipping the pistol Chaney had given her into her reticule. "I'll keep that in mind."

They stepped into the dropshaft.

"I can't believe you still have your reticule."

Tira ignored his comment. "I suppose you know what you're doing."

"I suppose I do, too, but I'm not real sure quite yet."

"I beg your pardon?"

"You're all so cocky and above-it-all, it's a wonder the High Secretary can see far enough down to sign his name to his documents."

Tira regarded Lieutenant Chaney with petulance. "How can you talk about my father that way?"

"Because I don't know him? Because I don't understand him? Come on. Does anyone know him?" asked Chaney.

"Yes, because you don't know him, or understand him. You don't know what he goes through every day for . . . Well, people don't."

"No, they don't. And for all I know, the Empire really couldn't function without him. That's what they all say. Nobody sees it, but they believe it. And they see how splendidly the High Secretary lives, and how splendidly he entertains, and how those in favor advance more swiftly than those who are not in favor."

Tira said nothing for a short while. "The assassins weren't rebels, not the kind you hear about on the news," she said a short while later. "Jessine wants the right and the power. You know the kind of man Ver is, and what she's like. They're ambitious. They *enjoy* palace coups." She shifted her position as much as her harness would let her. "Jessine. I hope she's stopped. I want her stopped right now." Her determination wilted. "My father. My brother. She got them both." She averted her face and began to weep. "Twenty-four, that's all she is. And she got them both."

For a little while, Chaney left her alone. He was never very good with crying women.

Chapter 2

As Tira sped away from the Secretary's Palace, her father's second wife stretched out above her long-time lover, Damien Ver. The ancient cameo hanging from a thong around her neck was slick with sweat, wine, and perfumed oil. Ver had given Jessine the pendant after their second meeting, when he was sure how he felt about her. She wore it to please him —

To please him in one of the ways they continued to please each other.

She arched her body, feeling the first tingle of approaching orgasm. Her face changed as she moved, softening to a sensual innocence that only two men ever saw. She looked down at Ver, her anticipation delicious. The profile on the cameo matched Ver's.

Damien Ver was a very attractive man when he was acting human. As the head of the Kona Tatsu, he generally presented a cold and forbidding persona to those unfortunate enough to come to his attention. They all thought he was more like a machine than a man. No one was aware of his passion for Jessine, intense but without obsession. He knew he could never have more of her than he had already, so he'd stopped tormenting himself.

Jessine's room was made for this, for sensual delight and seduction. The appointments were soft, highlighting Jessine's own softness. All the servo units were discreetly hidden, highly ornamented or disguised. The light was filmy, the scent was exciting, the music caressed the senses. Underneath the caressing drapes was technology that, if necessary, could run a full military surveillance post.

"Da . . . Dam . . . ien."

His hands slid up her body, reaching up to pull them close together. Nothing he had ever touched gave him the sheer depth of pleasure Jessine did, no one he had ever mounted had opened herself to passion the way she did. She was more than remarkable, she was bright as truth. Since they had been lovers, her passion for him had only increased.

Just as his fever peaked, his AID sent him a sharp tone. His transformation was abrupt and comprehensive. Hands frozen against Jessine's ribs, he focused on the incoming information.

Urgent, insisted the AID. *The High Secretary has been assassinated.* Ver winced inside, though he knew Jessine couldn't hear the intelligencer. *Acknowledged,* he responded, then murmured a few reassuring words to Jessine. Her movements against him had stopped as she sensed his sudden distraction.

"What is it?" she asked. She clutched him tighter. "My husband?"

He paused before answering her, focusing on the flow of information from his AID. "Yes. Your husband." Finally the flow stopped and he left her embrace. Kneeling beside her on the bed, he kissed her, long and deep. "Guard yourself, Jessine. It could be dangerous." He began to gather up his uniform, scattered around the chamber. Then he changed his mind and took a small pack of ordinary clothes out of the closet, where it had waited next to skiing togs and riding habits.

"Tell me," she pleaded, reaching out to grab his sleeve.

"When I have confirmed . . . " Someone else would have to tell her — not he. He would die for her if necessary. But he could not tell her she was a widow.

"Damien —"

He caught her hand in his and deliberately kissed her fingers. "Not now, Jessine. Not until I know for sure. In the mean time we have to get you away from here." He broke away from her, going toward the bathroom. He would have to wash and dress in less than two minutes if he wanted to stay ahead of the chaos. As he went through a hurried shower, he thought of the two best bolt-holes he knew of. Machines shaved and dried him; he was just fastening his shoes when the sirens began to whoop. He moved more quickly as new information came through.

"I heard," said Jessine as Ver came through her bedchamber.

"I'll send my men. They'll protect you. I'd stay but —"

"I know." She gave him a single, swift kiss and she motioned him away.

Then he left and the enormity of her predicament came home to her. If her assumption was right and the High Secretary was dead, the Empire would fall into chaos. In dismay she set about putting her things together, trying to anticipate how much she would need and for how long. She chose her clothing for rigorous practicality, including the three strands of almond-sized Milurean tsarovite which might buy her escape, if it came to that.

She had no wish to be at the center of a power vacuum when the winds began to fill it. Little as she wanted to admit it, she was frightened. With Ver gone, all she had to protect her was her mute alien staff, selected for their silence and discretion, not their skill at arms. She paced around her fantasy of a room, ignoring its sensual promises. At the window she looked down nervously, anticipating the arrival of rebel squads. She didn't know what faction would take advantage of the confusion first, but she knew Damien Ver was keeping an eye on one particular admiral with ambition.

If only there was someone in the building she could trust. That was the worst thing about this. The alien staff would do their jobs as long as her position appeared viable. She was not certain that the aliens would protect her once armed men arrived. They had no reason to defend her. She doubted she could trust them. She doubted she could trust anyone.

A discreet knock at the inner door caught her attention. For a moment, she stared at the door. Then she picked up the small railgun concealed in the door of an armoire. She strapped it to her hand and wrist before checking the spy hole.

Kitchley stood at the door, his golden alien face set in lines that Jessine recognized as concern. A native of Daphne, Kitchley had served as the Appointments Clerk to the High Secretary for years and was so familiar a presence that he hardly seemed alien any longer. Originally little more than a butler, time and proficiency had turned Kitchley into a power in his own right. Although few would think of him as such, he was undoubtedly the most influential bureaucrat in the Pact.

Jessine opened the door and stared at him, unsure what to say, not knowing his assessment of the crisis.

"I am very sorry, Lady Jessine, for your loss, and for the danger you face at present." His voice had an odd timbre, as if he were speaking on two tones at once, one deep and ragged, the other higher and smooth.

"Thank you," she said, thinking, *confirmation.*

He's gone. Sadness cut a narrow stream through her tension.

"I know it must be a great shock to you," he said gently. "Your kind are always deeply upset at the death of those close to you."

"Yes, I suppose . . . yes," she said, realizing that she had given her husband no more than a passing worry. "I don't think I can have taken it in yet."

"Probably not," said Kitchley. "I am making arrangements to get you out of here. I don't want you to have any more trouble." His nod was courtly.

"What do you mean?" Jessine asked, feeling disoriented.

"I am arranging for an escort. It will take you to my vacation home in Horizon Park: the estate is fortified and patrolled. No one will suspect you are there. You will be safe until we can reestablish order." He smoothed his long tunic, his six-fingered hand moving quickly, holding her attention.

"That is very good of you, but I don't want you to put yourself at risk. This isn't a Daphne matter." She saw approval in his amber eyes. She decided she would rather go with Kitchley now than await whatever Ver planned.

"I have my own position to protect. Not many

aliens have advanced as far as I have," Kitchley said. True enough, and Jessine certainly understood what he intended.

"I would be grateful for your protection. If we both survive and I have the power to do it, I will reward you." She tried to smile, then gave it up as a bad idea. It was enough to assure him that his service would not go unappreciated. He nodded acknowledgment.

"You have a weapon." He indicated the small railgun.

"Yes. And there's a pistol in my hovercraft, if we can get to it, and extra ammunition." She secured the wrist bands of her anorak. "Do we leave yet?"

"Not without the escort," said Kitchley. "We need them. You and I are too well-known. We are apt to be recognized. They will be here in ten minutes, or not at all. We will decide what to do about that if we must." He watched the windows and the security display. "So far there are no intruders near us."

"How long can that last?" She flexed her hands, needing to move. "Admiral Sclerida's troops are likely to arrive at any moment."

"Sclerida?" said Kitchley. "Do you mean he's behind this?" He stared as if he truly did not believe her.

She returned his stare. "Well, who else? The Haiken Maru conglomerate supports Senator Lomax, and he's certainly ambitious — but why would he do something this drastic when it could mean losing his own power?"

"But — Sclerida?"

It was not in Jessine to reveal her sources. "You know how it is — you overhear things, you're told things at parties and receptions by men who wish to impress you. I would have thought that Admiral Sclerida was the most likely conspirator, what with having all of Naval Logistics at his beck and call. He's greedy enough, and he's been trying for years to bring the High Secretary under his influence. So far unsuccessfully."

Kitchley nodded. "Yes. Exactly. An obvious choice; perhaps too obvious. But don't you see, he's not in the same position as Senator Lomax. Lomax has all the power of the biggest conglomerate in the empire behind him."

"I still think it must be Sclerida," said Jessine. "If he *is* the one, then all ships must be regarded as hostile." She shuddered. "To lose the Navy to a coup — that's frightening."

Kitchley interrupted. "I don't believe he controls the Protectorate, only Logistics."

Jessine's eyes narrowed as she worked out the

implications. "We would still be completely unprotected off Earth. If you're right, and the Haiken Maru are with the rebellion . . ." Now she steeled herself, thinking of Ver and hearing her own doubts about him at the same instant. "I hope that the Kona Tatsu are loyal. We need at least one force to remain with us if we're to survive. If they go over to the rebels, then — "

"Then we will have to arrange to leave the planet as soon as possible," said Kitchley.

"Yes," said Jessine, wondering if that would make any difference.

"We'll get you safe. Don't worry," Kitchley assured her, glancing apprehensively at the ornate wall clock.

A sudden crashing knock on the main door to her suite jolted them both. They exchanged glances as the battering continued.

"Check the screens," recommended Kitchley. "Keep them on opaque, one way view only."

"Of course," she said, irritated. "God of the Cosmos!" she whispered as the wall in front of her shifted to screen mode.

There was a squad of well-armed Cernian aliens in the corridor. Jessine's breath caught in her throat. "That's not your escort, right?"

Kitchley looked frightened. "No," he squeaked.

Over the announcing scanner came the order,

"Open up in the name of the High Secretary. We are ordered to secure these premises."

Jessine recovered. "I don't think so," she whispered. "They're with the rebels."

Kitchley didn't disagree.

The Cernians brought their heavy repulsors to bear. Under close range heavy barrage, the wall shuddered, then seemed to melt.

"Perhaps we should leave now," offered Kitchley.

Jessine broke for the living room and the hidden dropshaft.

Kitchley started to follow, still watching the wall-screen. Then the Cernians turned away from the wreckage of the wall. A squad of human troops in plain black uniforms came into the corridor, railguns at the ready.

"Look!" Kitchley called to Jessine.

"*You* look," said Jessine, staring out the window in horror. Two armored troop carriers hovered in the central quad.

Kitchley turned, the enormity of their problem becoming abundantly clear. "That is *not* my escort. How did they manage?"

"Inside help, or they've taken more of the complex than we realized," Jessine replied, still staring.

"Down!" Jessine dropped to the floor, one

hand dragging Kitchley's sleeve. She dared not raise her head to see if he was safe. The window vanished with a crash.

The black snout of one of the APC's poked through the empty window. Laser-cannon set in the turret moved restlessly, for all the world like antennae. Still on the floor, Jessine tried to wriggle backwards, away from the advancing vessel.

Kitchley checked the wall screen. The black-clad guards were making for the inner door.

Jessine climbed to her feet and tried again to reach the hidden dropshaft. Kitchley rolled under a claw-footed couch. The first man into the room from the APC grabbed for Jessine, his hand just brushing her tunic. She let her breath out. She was going to make it. Then a line of red light flashed between her and the dropshaft. She stopped short, stumbling, and the man had her.

Damn! But she gained her balance again. Moving with his pull on her arm, Jessine swung her fist back into the soldier's groin. She felt her hand bruise against the shell of his cup. The soldier grunted, but didn't let go. Jessine kept turning, her right hand coming up and around. As her head turned and she saw his face shield, she speared her hand at his throat. This time, he let go. But the other guards were on them. There were too many, and Jessine was overwhelmed and carried back toward the window. The Cernians were in the next room and the walls were starting to tremble.

The side bay door of the APC slid open and soldiers inside reached out to grab her. More soldiers swarmed around her, forcing her through the door. Below them a second troop carrier was holding off soldiers on the ground.

The Cernians had almost destroyed a second interior wall and were now training their weapons on the troop carrier.

The troop carrier's turret laser-cannon swung around and fired a short burst into the center of the Cernians.

Three of the Cernians were shattered by direct hit, bits of their uniforms and flesh flung about the room in sizzling, pulsing heaps. The others drew back out of the room.

"Get out of here," one of the officers ordered, and the troop carrier slid back from the wreckage of Jessine's suite, to hover over the other troop carriers in the quad. "And take care of Merimee."

"Who the hell do you think you are?" demanded Jessine.

A tall young man pushed his way through his men. "Lieutenant Varrick of the Kona Tatsu, Madame Merimee. Our orders are to get you to safety."

Jessine was seldom called by her maiden name these days, and that caught her attention even as she was pushed firmly into an acceleration couch.

Lieutenant Varrick secured the final buckles. "Just lie back and relax, Madame. You can't do anything for the High Secretary now. Leave it to us."

"Who sent you?" she demanded.

"Damien Ver," said the lieutenant.

The answer left Jessine with more questions, but none she thought Lieutenant Varrick could answer.

"Opponent approaching. Opponent approaching," declared the carrier's computer voice. "Directly above."

"Above?" repeated Varrick as a shadow came over them.

"Opponent identified," the computer said calmly. "Naval assault frigate, Logistics garrison."

"Logistics? Sclerida!" Jessine slapped at the harness release and launched herself from the couch. She shoved through the packed men to the open bay. "Oh my God!"

"Nav, evasive action," ordered Varrick. "Comm, I don't suppose they're hailing us."

The hail came direct from a loudspeaker. "Troop carrier. Troop carrier. This is your order to surrender. Repeat, this is your order to surrender. You are out-manned and out-gunned. Surrender now and no harm will come to you. All we want is the Lady Jessine."

"If we let her go, Ver will take us apart a joint at a time," muttered Varrick. He glanced back at Jessine. "Demoiselle, strap in. This might get bouncy."

"So how about that safety, Lieutenant?" said Jessine, strapping back into her couch.

"We're doing what we can, Madame," said Varrick.

"Troop carrier, surrender. You have thirty seconds to surrender." The frigate's hailer was impossibly loud, and the soldiers made faces at this order.

"Men," said the lieutenant. "Ready short-range weapons. Be ready to fire at any angle, any time. Go for their stabilizers and power ducts. Helm, where's that evasive action? Get moving."

The APC swung onto its side and slipped away from the frigate, running almost parallel to the fortieth-floor windows of the Palace.

The frigate came around in an arc, not as agile as the troop carrier, but more lethal. Its first shot hit the APC's navigational complex, and the rear of the craft began to yaw.

"Frigging bastards!" snarled Lieutenant Varrick. As he watched, the frigate came around again. The APC was still swinging from the last attack.

Jessine closed her eyes, then opened them again immediately. There was nothing she wanted to look at, but she didn't want to look at nothing. Her hands gripped the arms of the acceleration couch. It would take so little for the troop carrier to spin out of control and plummet into the quad below.

"All troops!" shouted Varrick as the frigate approached. "Fire at will!"

The frigate closed. Its guns fired in series, and one side of the troop carrier tore off and fell away, burning. The scream of wounded metal couldn't mask the cries of falling men. Huge sections of metal and plastic sailed away like kites on the wind. Two pieces struck the windows of the Secretary's Palace, adding the brilliance of shattered glass to the debris.

The APC swung wildly, half its fans reduced to scrap metal. The vehicle dropped sickeningly fast despite the red-lined efforts of the remaining ducts. The navigator and helmsmen swore continuously as they fought for control of the ship, trying to ease it into the quad. Jessine braced in crash position and tried to relax her muscles.

Will I know when we hit? she wondered. *Or*

will there just be nothing? She hoped it would be nothing, but in this buffered fall there might still be a chance of landing without killing damage.

Then Jessine saw the second APC swoop up past them, guns coming around to take on the frigate. Seconds later, she heard an enormous explosion, then felt the shock. *We've hit ground*, she thought. But they were still falling. The noise continued, accompanied by debris falling on her APC from above. Then they did hit, and Jessine blacked out.

Chapter 3

It had turned into an outdoor party, with most of the cocky young aristocrats taking to their air-cars for a little sport with the groundlings. Up until the time that the game had been suggested, Wiley Bouriere, the High Secretary's son, was pretty bored, but now he felt excitement and the thrill of the hunt. He had not gone out after groundlings for several months — he had been forbidden by his father, a restriction he found more than normally irksome.

"Let's go to Undertown," yelled Caroly Rhodi, who knew more about this sport than most of them. "They've got shanties and trailers over there. And aliens. There's lots we can do."

His suggestion was greeted by cheers from everyone but the bodyguards. These exchanged silent, condemning looks.

"Undertown!" the others called out, racing toward their aircars. "Let's do Undertown!"

Garen McModor caught his lower lip between his teeth. Being bodyguard to Wiley Bouriere was awkward enough at the best of times, for the High Secretary's son resented the constant observation and often did his best to elude his security staff. But when he took off on strange quirks, McModor's job became truly perilous. Parties like this one, that could turn ugly in a pulse-beat, were McModor's least favorite of Wiley's pastimes. He signaled Wiley, wanting him to reconsider.

Wiley studiously ignored him, listening with exaggerated interest to what Caroly had to say. He knew already that McModor did not approve of these romps and he was not about to listen to another recitation of the danger he might be courting. "We can fill up bottles with paint, and fuel. That would make it more interesting," he suggested to Caroly.

"And guns. Let's take our guns," added Caroly, and turned to address the others. "We're going to Undertown," he announced grandly. "We'll use our aircars, yours and mine, Wiley, and Maytag's. We can all fit in three, can't we? No, we'll need a fourth. I know! Thistlewaite!" exclaimed Caroly, pointing to a gangly youth in a luminous skinsuit. "You have that spiffy Hovermaster tonight, don't you? Wiley and I will lead. You can follow us." He laughed wildly, and made a very rude gesture to his bodyguard. "Security can bring up the rear." This suggestion was in fact an order, which all of them understood. "I haven't been to Undertown for months and months," said Bentess Hull, flinging her mane of fashionably green hair about her shoulders, imitating the women in the vidis. "I miss it."

"They probably miss us, too," called out one half-drunk wag. Everyone laughed, except the bodyguards.

"Then let's get going," Caroly ordered, and set the example by gathering up glastic bottles and throwing them in a large sack.

"Better check your ammunition, too," warned Lolana Palomare, the hard look in her sandy-brown eyes making her smile unbelievable. "If we're taking pistols."

"You're right," said Wiley, wondering if Lolana would aim to miss the way the rest of them did.

And so the party became an interactive air tour of Undertown, where aliens and humans without jobs lived. Making up the group: four sports cars, high-priced; thirteen aristocratic teenagers, just plain high; and five patrol choppers, with nine bodyguards, highly stressed.

Wiley Bouriere's aircar was a very shiny brass Radeo 434 hyperlift with auxiliary stabilizers, the fastest and most maneuverable aircar available anywhere, and the envy of most of his friends. Caroly's was a red-and-silver Kahna World-walker, the 800 series with the aerobatic modifications. The two of them performed intricate braiding patterns as they rushed around the tall buildings, never both on the same street at the same time. Thistlewaite was an excellent driver, but his aircar was not as advanced as Wiley's and Caroly's, and he lagged behind. Maytag lacked such reckless nerve and tended to stick to right-angle turns, executed at unpredictable intervals. Neither Thistlewaite nor Maytag were as high as Wiley or Caroly, of course.

Caroly had Bentess Hull riding with him, acting as spotter, and a passenger, the brilliant and erratic Tonio van Lewat in the back.

Wiley was showing off the Radeo to his three cohorts. Dov Sclerida and his flamboyant girlfriend, Crisianne Nemor, rode in the back, Dov firing his pistol and throwing glue-filled bottles. His third passenger was a girl whose name Wiley thought might be Nika, a pretty thing with bronze hair who wasn't as into the partying as the others. Her idea of fun was a bit different. From time to time she reached over to take Wiley's hand and place it on her thigh, but he always ended up with both hands on the steering bar as he attempted another spectacular and dangerous stunt.

"Hey, look at that!" yelled Dov as he fired at a group of squat, four-legged aliens. They scattered as the aircar passed over them, the airpads stirring up half a dozen miniature tornadoes.

"Endorites," shrieked Crisianne, waving frantically as they passed over the group. They dropped four bottles of glowing paint on the shacks where the aliens lived. Her shrieks turned to giggles as the smallest of these collapsed, a brilliant purple sunflower blossoming atop the rubble.

Thistlewaite and Maytag had found a group of locals apparently playing some kind of game, and they harried the aliens, flying dangerously low to the ground to drive them to run. One of their victims threw a rock at Maytag's aircar and in the next instant one of Thistlewaite's passengers had dropped a bottle full of flaming brandy on his head.

Everyone in the aircars laughed as the local staggered and fell.

Wiley rushed the Radeo up the side of the nearest building, to the level where the successful aliens lived. Here, Wiley and his friends did nothing more than stare in windows, for, alien or human, at this level the inhabitants could not be attacked with impunity. The aircar did a spectacular slow roll, and then once again they hurtled toward the shanties of Undertown.

Dov fired three rounds as they leveled off just above the street. Then his ammunition was gone and he cursed the pistol before reaching for the last of the bottles to throw.

Caroly and his gang whizzed by, Tonio releasing bottles of fuel every six seconds, aiming for the sideways. Wiley could hear Caroly bellowing a popular song, trying to compete with the roar of his Worldwalker.

Another, larger aircar appeared ahead of Caroly, and behind it he could just make out a Navy assault boat, fully armed and blocking the intersection six blocks away. Wiley scowled. Who were they to interrupt his fun?

Caroly's Worldwalker balked suddenly, the rotors slowing. Caroly held the steering bar with all his strength, striving to keep the aircar from crashing. Only his autorotating fans allowed him to ride it down to the ground. He heard Tonio yell something, and then they banged into the street.

Wiley stared at the wreck of Caroly's aircar. He realized Caroly was down at the levels they had just buzzed, with no weapons. There would be locals waiting. Then looked down the street in the opposite direction: another assault boat was closing in on them. More irked than worried, Wiley yelled to Dov Sclerida, "What's your father up to now?" He had to hold the steering bar in this narrow street and could not point out the assault boats.

"What are you talking about?" asked Dov, dropping a bottle of stinkbalm over the side.

"Navy assault boats," said Wiley, nodding in the direction of the nearest. "I make out six so far."

"I don't —" Dov began, then broke off in alarm. "Where'd they come from?" he demanded as if someone was deliberately withholding the answer.

"Look at them," whispered Wiley, his pleasant intoxication fading rapidly. "What do they want?"

The girl beside him reached over and grabbed

his leg, for once without any seductive intent, her fingers gouging his muscles.

Catching up with his charge's group at last, Wiley's chief bodyguard eyed the assault boats from the far end of the street. Perhaps these children could be persuaded to find more suitable entertainment. Though six Navy assault boats seemed a lot to discipline a baker's dozen of unruly adolescents. He hailed the assault boats.

"McModor here, from the Secretary's Guard," he sent. "Come to fetch the Sclerida boy?"

There was no response.

"I'm not reading anything off them," said his second. "No hull signals, nothing."

"This doesn't feel right." McModor hit the send key again. "Lieutenant McModor of the Secretary's Guard, hailing Naval assault boat, please respond."

The answer this time came from the boat's guns.

Two blocks over, another assault boat brought down Thistlewaite's aircar without a single shot. The revelers were weak with apprehension as they saw the huge boats open their hatches.

Not far away, Maytag did his best to get away

and in a sudden blazing miscalculation slammed into the side of the building.

Ahead Wiley's aircar wobbled and dropped down onto the street.

Wiley sat, more dazed from the jarring impact than anything he had consumed earlier that evening. "McModor?" For once he was wishing the guard would show up. Yell at him, anything. Anything normal. But McModor was nowhere in sight and he became aware of the locals, watching, perhaps waiting for a chance to exact some vengeance. He fumbled with the harness release, his fingers refusing to cooperate. Finally, he broke free of the harness and scrambled out of the useless aircar. The girl who had been sitting with him followed on his heels.

In the rear seat Dov and Crisianne struggled to get free of the restraining harnesses.

Half a block away one assault boat had landed and a dozen men in Navy uniform came toward them, stunguns on their hips. From the hatch the long pointed beaks of laser-cannon pointed out at the four young roisterers.

"Come on, Bouriere," said one of the men as he reached Wiley. "Sorry to do it this way, but we have to bring you in." He took a firm hold on Wiley's arm just above the elbow and began to lead Wiley toward the assault boat.

Wiley blinked in disbelief at this treatment. "I'm the High Secretary's son," he began, and heard his voice rise sharply. He tried again. "I'm the High Secretary's son."

"We know that," said another one of the Navy men brusquely, escorting the girl who had been sitting beside Wiley in the aircar.

Never before had Wiley had this announcement fail. He tried to draw himself up, but before he could get more than two words out, the man who held him said, "Look, son, that's all changing. It's changing right now. You might as well get used to it." There was a hint of apology in the man's voice.

"Changing?" Wiley echoed, beginning to be deeply afraid.

Nika was oddly calm, taking in these announcements as if she had expected to hear them.

"What about Dov?" As Wiley spoke his friend's name he looked around. Dov and Crisianne were being taken to another assault boat, also accompanied by armed guards. "Where are you taking him? Why isn't he with us?"

"Look," said another of the men. "You let us do our job, everything'll be fine."

"But Dov —" Wiley protested.

"We have orders," said his escort. "Nothing personal."

They were almost at the assault boat, and the man leading the girl said, "Are we supposed to bring her, or leave her here?"

"I don't know," admitted Wiley's captor. "They didn't say anything about her." He blinked once. "We might as well bring her."

"What if they don't want her?" asked the man guarding her.

"Let them decide. It's not up to us to figure them out." He nudged Wiley toward the lowered steps. "Better get in. And nothing fancy. You can't get out of here even if you want to."

Of that Wiley was absolutely certain. He thought for one heady moment of breaking away and running for safety. But there was no safety; if the Navy men didn't catch him, the locals would. He made a gesture of acquiescence. "Sure." He started to climb, his legs feeling unsteady.

Behind him the girl started up the steps, her movements more graceful, more controlled than Wiley's. She looked hard at the man who had led her, as if she wanted to remember his face.

There were another twenty men in the assault boat, and they went about their chore of adjusting racks for Wiley and the girl, saying very little as they did. Then the hatch was closed and secured.

Nika lost her footing as the straps were adjusted, and fell against Wiley.

As she did, Wiley felt the sting of an injection. He stared at his arm where she had touched him, trying to convince himself he had imagined it. Why should she inject him? And what would she inject him with? The second question remained stuck in his mind like a splinter of ice refusing to melt.

The engines bellowed and the assault car lifted into the air. Wiley could feel the back and forth movement as it maneuvered to avoid colliding with the other boats.

Then there was a faintly pink fog filling the boat, smelling of rotting hay and unripe apples. Wiley could see that the fog came from something on the girl's belt, from a strangely wrought cylinder Wiley had assumed was a piece of jewelry.

The Navy men noticed the fog about two seconds before they collapsed. One moment they were standing at their posts, and then they crumpled like marionettes with cut strings.

Wiley held his breath, expecting to lose consciousness at any moment.

The assault boat began to yaw.

Nika unfastened the catches of her rack and hurried toward the pilot's station. She dragged the pilot from his chair, dumping him on the deck before sliding into place. She grabbed the control bar with both hands, fighting to bring the assault boat back on course. Her eyes flicked over the instrument panel with the habit of familiarity.

Staring at her, Wiley asked, "Who are you?"

"Get out of the rack and give me a hand," she said. "We've got to get clear of this place as quickly as possible."

"What's going on?" Wiley fumbled with the rack harness. "What did you do to them?"

"Poison gas. I gave you the antidote before," she said, watching the forward screen with intense concentration.

Wiley studied her for a moment. She seemed suddenly older, more a woman than the girls he knew. He was out of the rack now, but he hesitated to approach her. If only he knew who she was, or why she was here.

"Get the copilot out of there and harness yourself in," she commanded. "Now."

Wiley did as she ordered. He shoved the Navy pilot into a corner, thinking as he did that the woman must have some special reason for what she was doing. He wondered if she was working for his side — whichever side that was — or against his side. Was he free or was he a hostage?

The communications board lit up and the other assault boat signaled them. "Anything wrong over there?"

"Answer them," said Nika. "Say we had a sheer."

Wiley found the switch and told the other boat they had a sheer.

"Report status," came back the response.

Wiley looked at Nika a little wildly. "Now what?"

"Say uncertain." Her pretty face was stern now, and Wiley thought, *If I'm being kidnapped, at least I'm being kidnapped by a beautiful woman.*

"Uncertain," he relayed.

"Brace yourself." She eased the huge ship up through the narrow canyon between buildings.

The other assault boat came abreast of them, so close that the air rocked and boiled between the two boats.

Nika nudged the assault boat to higher speeds. "We can't fight here," she muttered.

The second assault boat grew nearer, and Wiley noticed that a third had turned to follow them.

They raced through the streets, moving away from the most densely populated part of the city. Now the buildings were less tightly packed. With the increased maneuvering room, the second assault boat brought its laser-cannon into firing position.

Nika fired all four of her cannon directly into the inertial guidance pod of the second boat. She took advantage of the chaos to put more distance between herself and the third assault boat.

"We're getting away," said Wiley, not sure if this was supposed to please him or not.

"No," said Nika. "There're another five boats out there. We just bought a little time, that's all." She set most of the controls on automatic and got out of the pilot's harness. "Come on."

Wiley stared at her. "What?"

"Come on, let's go. We've got to get out while we can. They'll cut us off or shoot us down in another two minutes if we don't leave now. Get *moving*." She dragged a full parachute pack out of the locker and tugged on the harness. "Hurry up."

"But — " Wiley protested. Surely the assault boat was safer than a parachute.

"They're going to start firing on us any second now," she told him bluntly as she started to the hatch release. "I've got a smoke canister rigged; we'll have a little cover while we drop."

"Uh — " said Wiley.

She reached out and tugged him toward the hatch. "There's no time, Bouriere."

Already the third assault boat was getting closer. He nodded and started to reach for a second parachute.

"No time," said Nika as she threw the hatch open. She locked her arms around Wiley and secured him with the rescue latch.

She stepped out into nothing as the assault boat began to pour out two colors of smoke.

The air buffeted them as they fell, and they rocked violently as the first of the two 'chutes opened. Nika secured the control shrouds; they slid between two buildings and out of the line of sight of the pursuing assault boats.

Behind them an explosion blossomed.

As they neared the ground, Nika noticed that they had not yet moved beyond the city limits. She swore.

"What's the matter?" demanded Wiley. He paled as they fell past the side of a building. He thought he could count the bricks, if he'd had time.

"We're still inside the city," she said, shouting to be heard against the rush of the wind. "If I hadn't had to outrun that second boat, we'd be outside the limits."

"And?" Wiley asked.

"I've missed the drop point," she said, and swore with a thoroughness any Navy officer would envy.

They were almost on the ground.

Wiley still had no idea who she was.

Chapter 4

Lieutenant Chaney was muttering again.

"What is it?" asked Tira, feeling slightly dazed. As they were floating down the drop shaft, she had let her mind drift so she wouldn't have to think about the future.

He held up a hand, listening. "Help. My uncle. We're to skip the guard room and go to the sub-basement garage. Someone will meet us."

"Your uncle?" asked Tira dubiously.

"Commander Kenigern Chaney."

"Ah," said Tira, feeling no wiser. "And what do we do in the sub-basement?"

"Wait," responded Chaney. "For reinforcements."

They fell past several floors, Tira growing uneasy. Finally, one stop before the sub-basement, she grabbed at Chaney's arm.

"We're getting off here." She tugged and they stepped out of the shaft.

"What? Why? Uncle Ken said . . ."

"I know what Uncle Ken said. But Uncle Ken isn't here and I am." Tira glared at Chaney. "Whose rescue is this, anyway?"

"I *thought* it was mine, of you," grumbled Chaney under his breath. "Now what, Demoiselle? We still have to get down to the rendezvous."

Tira wasn't so sure about that, but she wasn't sure what *else* to do. At least her change in plans would give them a chance to see the "reinforcements" before they saw her.

"We can walk down the stairs."

"All right, then." He looked around. The dropshaft fell in the middle of one wall. "Left or right?" he asked. "There are fire stairs in each corner. Just pick one."

"Left," Tira said, and set off briskly. She felt exposed under the bright ceiling lights.

They'd reached the stairwell and started down when a noise on the floor below caught Chaney's attention. He motioned Tira to be still and ran the rest of the way down. Leaning up against the stairwell wall, he tried to see through the window in the door.

"Dear God," he whispered in shock. He raced back up the stairs, grabbing Tira's arm as he passed her.

"Cernians," he hissed. "Dozens of them."

"Looking for us," Tira said. She let his hand stay on her arm.

"Looking for *you*. We'll have to try something else." His lips continued to move as he subvocalized instructions to his AID.

They were not quite two full flights up when a door opened and a Treasury guard entered the stairwell above them. He shouted, lifting his gun to fire.

Chaney shoved Tira back against the wall, out of the direct line of fire. Pulling his pistol from its holster, he returned fire. The Treasury guard fell, blocking open the door. A wild thought ran through Chaney's mind: move the guard, close the door, head up the stairs again . . . but he could hear more guards coming closer already.

He checked his ammunition — seventy-nine rounds in the weapon and two spare clips. Okay. Better than nothing.

"Who is it?" Tira asked.

"Same as before." Two shots punctuated Chaney's answer as the Treasury men commenced firing.

"We're pinned down," he told her. "Pick your targets and don't give up. I've called for help."

Tira nodded, and took her pistol from her reticule.

There was more firing now, and the first indication of a bustle in the sub-basement as well, as the Cernians responded to the sound of gunfire.

Chaney found what he thought was the most protected place in the stairwell, a few steps down from the upper landing, but on the high side of the switchback from the lower landing. Both the Treasury men and the Cernians would have to expose themselves to get a clear shot at Chaney and Tira. They squatted down against the railing and kept firing.

There was a heavy thud as at least one of the aliens fell back.

Chaney hoped he had hit him badly enough to take him out of the fight. If help didn't come soon, he and Tira had little or no chance to get out. Out-numbered and cut off, eventually they would run out of ammunition. He wondered if he should save two shots, just in case.

Tira was firing more frequently and with longer bursts, but didn't seem to have inflicted any serious damage. "They're still coming," she whispered to Chaney.

"Keep shooting. Pick your targets."

"Pick my targets," she said. "Right. I wish I didn't have such a selection to pick *from*." Taking a deep breath, she thought suddenly of the many times her brother had come after her with a water pistol. Her eyes focused, her finger squeezed, and a Treasury guard went down. A new predatory gleam came into her eye and she relaxed, the way a cat does just before springing.

"Watch out!" she yelled at Chaney. A Cernian poked his head around the switchback.

Chaney fired; the slug went in through the shoulder and came out south of the ribs. The Cernian collapsed on the switchback, providing a barrier.

The other Cernians made a run at the bottom of the shaft, forcing both Chaney and Tira to use ammunition keeping them at bay. Chaney was sharply aware that they had no spare clips for the A7mark923.

"It doesn't look good," whispered Tira, needing no denial or confirmation from Chaney.

"There're too many of them." She fired and one of the Treasury men screamed. She kept her aim steady with an effort of will, for she was getting very tired as well as growing queasy at the slaughter above and below her. There had been too much dying for one day.

From the sub-basement came an ominous clang, as if iron doors were being torn off their hinges. Chaney had to hold back a groan of despair as he heard it, for the Cernians took courage at the sound and once again pressed forward.

Tira shot another Treasury man.

Two Cernians surged into the stairwell, moving quickly and efficiently, one giving covering fire to the other as they reached the first three steps.

Then there was a sharp explosion, and the whole stairwell shuddered. The Cernians froze; above, the Treasury men faltered.

"What was that?" Tira whispered, the sound echoing unintelligibly through the stairwell.

"I don't know," said Chaney, hating to admit it.

"What are we going to do?"

"Play it by ear," he advised, not telling her that he still had two shots reserved for them if they were required.

The noise in the sub-basement grew louder

and then came the sharp report of a Kanovsky 40-09 Antipersonnel riot control gun.

"What the devil?" said Chaney aloud. He was pretty sure that none of the Cernians were carrying Kanovskys.

On the floor above the Treasury men moved back to more secure cover.

The Cernians were fighting again, but no longer with Chaney and Tira. They had turned to face a more formidable opponent.

Four Kanovskys were firing now, directly into the Cernians. Technically designed to wound rather than kill, the weapons were usually loaded with plastic riot control cartridges. But these guns had a more lethal purpose, and the Cernians paid full measure against their might.

In a matter of seconds only five Cernians were still standing, two of them wounded. They held their weapons reversed for surrender, and waited with the dumb amazement of defeat as a detachment of Marines in body armor came into view at the base of the stairwell.

"Lieutenant Chaney?" called one of the Marines, his voice hollow in the stairwell and body armor.

"Yes," said Chaney, lowering his gun.

"Sorry we didn't get here earlier," said the Marine to Chaney; he ignored Tira completely.

"So are we," said Chaney with real feeling, and turned to give his hand to Tira. "There are Treasury men above and —"

"That's been taken care of," said the Marine, then coughed. "It would be best if we get moving, Lieutenant. Right now." He waved his arm to indicate the carnage around them. "Don't you think?"

"Yeah," said Chaney as he felt Tira's hand close around his.

"Hurry." The Marine was already moving away.

Chaney turned to escort Tira down the stairs. "It's the cavalry. Well, the Marines, anyway." He offered her his arm.

Tira's fingers shook as she tucked the Samtoepoe A7mark923 back into her reticule. "About time." Her voice shook, too. She took Chaney's arm with as much dignity and poise as she could muster.

They were bundled into a closed unmarked car. Three of the Marines climbed in after them. A Navy officer, a commander, was driving. None of the men had anything to say to Tira, despite her repeated questions.

Their silence made Tira uncomfortable. She could feel the lack of respect the men had for her.

"I don't suppose *you* know where we're going?" she whispered to Chaney, not wanting these silent Marines to hear her uncertainty.

"Well, no," Chaney admitted as he adjusted himself against the padded seats. "But it's better than where we were."

"For the moment." It was late in the day and fatigue was catching up with her; it showed in the way she sat and the low level of irritation that possessed her.

The journey seemed to go on forever. The road narrowed as it climbed into the foothills. Outcroppings of boulders loomed up in the darkness like giants, and the left side of the road fell away into ravines and dry creek-beds.

"Pretty inhospitable," said Tira as she peered out the window. "What kind of installation is out in a wilderness like this?" She had not often been out of the city, and when she had been it was to patrolled and groomed recreational lands, not this forbidding section of the continent.

"A secret one," said Chaney.

Tira considered this. "You're probably right. My father is . . . *was* always talking about secret installations and bases. He said Admiral Sclerida favored them." Her expression darkened. "Admiral Sclerida —"

"Don't," warned Chaney with a hitch of his

elbow in the direction of the driver. "Who knows who's playing what game."

Tira sighed. "I hate this. No matter who's at the end of this ride, I'll be one kind of hostage or another."

Chaney answered carefully. "I don't think that's likely." He was trying to soothe his own conscience as well as offer comfort. He had just been following his uncle's orders. But for the last half hour it had been dawning on him that no one knew where they were, and that the daughter of the High Secretary — whether Cowper Bouriere was alive or not — was a real prize. Any number of ambitious men might want to get their hands on her.

The driver had turned on the headlights. Though they were set low and shielded, they offered a little safety on the twisting road. "It won't be much longer now," he volunteered to his passengers.

"Where are we going?" asked Tira.

The driver said nothing more.

"Look, if they were going to kill you, they didn't have to bring you out here," said Chaney reasonably. "They could have left us to the Cernians and the rest, back at the Palace." He wanted to feel reassured by these assertions, but found that he could not accept them without question.

"Unless they were holding out for their own advantage," said Tira darkly. "There might be something to gain for getting me . . . out of the way." She glanced down at her reticule, heartened by the knowledge that she still had the Samtoepoe A7mark923 resting inside it, among other necessities of life.

Chaney nodded in spite of himself. "Yeah. But this is Uncle Ken's doing. He's not the kind who would . . . well, he doesn't exploit his family that way."

Tira scowled. "Meaning he might want to make a pawn of me, but not if you're involved? I hope you're right." She went back to staring out the window. They had entered a long canyon, the road now nothing more than a single-lane track along the side of the steep walls.

"I remember seeing this area on the maps, back at school," she said. "It's usually labeled 'The Barrens.' I used to wonder what that meant, and why there weren't any cities here." She shivered. "Now I know."

"It's pretty forbidding," said Chaney, remembering the many times he had flown over this landscape during training, thinking it looked beautiful from the air.

She folded her arms. "I don't recall learning about any bases out here, except the scientific ones. You don't suppose we're going to one of those, do you?"

"I don't know," said Chaney with a trace of exasperation. "I'm as much in the dark as you are."

Tira sighed. "I know that," she said, making the words an apology.

Without warning, the car entered a tunnel. The driver added a second set of headlights, but that didn't really cut the gloom out the side window.

"Where is this?" Tira asked uneasily as they sped on. She could barely make out tiled walls.

For once the driver answered. "It's the entrance to the base, Miss Bouriere. We're almost there."

"Wherever there is," said Chaney, trying to conceal the sudden apprehension that had taken hold of him.

"Your uncle's base," said the driver. "I think we're expected."

Tira stared at Chaney. "What do you think?"

"I think I hope he's right about Uncle Ken being here," said Chaney with feeling.

The car pulled into a wide bay where a small escort of Navy personnel waited, all in battle dress. As the car stopped the nearest of these men reached forward and opened the door for Chaney and Tira.

"Good evening, Lieutenant," he said very politely. "And to you, Miss Bouriere." He indicated the surroundings. "Sorry we had to resort to this, but we had to guarantee your safety."

"Thanks," said Chaney, getting out and holding his hand out for Tira. "We were beginning to wonder."

"Of course, of course," said the Navy officer. "You'll have questions. Just as we have answers." He closed the car door and saluted. "If you'll follow me, we'll escort you. This is a pretty confusing place until you learn your way around."

"And are we going to do that?" Tira inquired sweetly.

Chaney recognized a tone in her voice that the young officer evidently missed. He replied seriously. "It might come to that."

"I see," said Tira, and clutched her reticule more tightly. She did not look at Chaney.

The officer was right — the base was confusing. As they followed him through the halls, Chaney was quickly disoriented, and decided he would have a great deal of trouble finding his way back to the bay. He suspected that the young officer was making the route as complex as possible. No matter. His AID was in inertial tracking mode and better than a map with arrows.

"Where are you taking us?" he asked when they had gone some distance in silence.

"It's not far now," said the young officer, and turned the corner into a large hall. At the far end was a platform. On that platform stood a white-haired, straight-backed officer in a formal uniform that lacked rank tabs.

Chaney stood still as he took this in. Then he raised his voice. "Uncle Ken! Uncle Ken!" He started toward the platform, Tira tagging along behind him.

The man turned, smiling in welcome. "Yon!" he called. "At last."

Chaney was half-way to the platform now. "Thank God you're all right. It's been pretty hectic out there."

"I can imagine," said Uncle Ken, and his smile faded.

"What is it?" Chaney asked, closing the gap between them. "What's going on?"

Uncle Ken looked around, indicating with a gesture that this was not the place for such a discussion. He addressed the escort. "Thank you, Bycroft, you may leave now."

"As you wish," said the young officer, saluting briskly before turning his men and exiting from the conference hall quickly.

"If you two will come with me," said Uncle

Ken thoughtfully, "I think we can explain everything. Demoiselle Bouriere, I know you must be worried for your family." His sympathy seemed genuine enough, but Tira hung back from Uncle Ken, placing more faith in the man she knew.

There was a side door and Uncle Ken led them through it while discussing the size of the underground installation. "There's quite a complex above us, on the surface, but it's nothing like this."

"What *is* on the surface?" asked Tira.

"I thought I told you," said Uncle Ken as they entered yet another short hallway. "There's a large complex of administrative buildings."

"In the middle of the desert?" said Tira.

"Room is precious, even in this part of the planet," said Uncle Ken, ushering them into a side room.

Four Navy men were waiting, and they stepped up to Chaney, confining his arms and taking his pistol.

"What the devil . . . !" Chaney burst out. He struggled, trying to strike out at the four men.

Uncle Ken shook his head in commiseration. "I'm sorry, my boy, truly sorry. But you've gotten too deep in something you should have avoided. You cannot be allowed to interfere." He started to add something when a loud report filled the room.

There was a smoking hole in the side of Tira's reticule, and a much larger, bleeding one at the base of Uncle Ken's ribs. She stepped aside as Uncle Ken collapsed, and carefully pulled the Samtoepoe A7mark923 into view. "I think," she said very calmly, "that you had better let him go."

Chapter 5

Jessine blinked. She felt as though her internal clock had been set to zero. But the sounds of battle raged on outside, so she couldn't have been out long. She leaned against the harness she had fought so vigorously and gave it a grateful pat. She became aware of the bubble of silence within the storm and looked around, hesitantly.

Broken bodies were flung about the APC. Some of the men were still alive; she could hear their ragged breathing, but she couldn't tell which ones by looking. *So much death!* she thought. She stepped gingerly over the bodies, wishing her touch could heal.

"Madame . . ." It was Lieutenant Varrick, still at his command. "Madame . . . I've got to get you safe . . ." His voice trailed off.

She stepped over to his side, stroked his forehead, smearing her hand with his blood. "I'm safe," she lied, not knowing why. "Good work, Lieutenant."

"Safe . . . Ver will . . ."

"I'm safe, Lieutenant. Damien will know."

Lieutenant Varrick closed his eyes. Jessine didn't know if he'd believed her.

She certainly knew better. Varrick's — or Ver's — plan had failed. She needed a new one, now. Most of the port side of the ship had been blasted away, giving plenty of room for Jessine to escape, but she hesitated. The battle was still going on and she could see that the whole of the Secretary's Palace was in an uproar. She needed to make herself less obvious if she were to have a chance of getting away.

One of the dead soldiers had a long, loose field-poncho over his uniform, a garment of steelcloth, of a color so neutral that it made its wearer hard to see. Reaching down, she pulled and tugged at the field-poncho, trying to get it off the body. The task was more difficult than she had thought it would be. But the continuing sound of gunfire and explosions kept her at it until she felt the corpse release the garment.

Another clatter of gunfire sounded just outside the crashed ship, and Jessine froze for an instant. With shaking hands she shrugged out of her designer anorak and slipped on the poncho, hating the smell of death that clung to it. Bending down, she dipped her hand into the dead soldier's clotting blood. She rubbed her arm with it and smeared a little along her cheekbone. Then she pulled the little Ridly 20-44 from the soldier's holster and checked the magazine. Bracing herself, she rifled her dead soldier and his companions for spare magazines. Finding four, she tucked them into her belt and lowered the field-poncho over it. The gun she kept in her hand.

In the far side of the quadrangle a gaggle of Emergency Service personnel were starting to run toward the wrecked ship, a few carrying life-paks, the others with guns. Gunfire sent up little sprays of paving and dust around them as they ran.

Emerging from the ship, Jessine stumbled

deliberately in order to enhance the illusion she was wounded. She started toward the central pylon of the Secretary's Palace, the field-poncho flapping as she ran. As she had hoped, no one paid much attention to her.

There should have been an automatic walkway running through the central garden, but it was stopped. Most of the plants had been blasted or trampled and of the three ornamental fountains, only one had a trickle of water coming from its decapitated Nike.

Jessine ran down the halted walkway. Kitchley's office was nineteen floors above her in what had once been a diplomatic reception room, but had been pressed into service as office space more than twenty years ago. She decided to head for that.

Jessine avoided the dropshafts. The civilian ones might not be dependable, and she lacked the codes for the military ones. Her husband had never involved his twenty-four-year-old bride in military affairs. No matter. She didn't want an entrance that wouldn't allow quick exit. That left the stairs or the old-fashioned freight lifts. She tried to remember where the lifts were.

There was a cross hallway some distance ahead of her, and Jessine slowed down, listening for what she might encounter.

A squad of Treasury fighters came jogging along in loose formation, a sergeant urging them on. He slowed as he caught sight of Jessine. "Trouble, soldier?" he shouted.

Jessine held up her bloody arm. "I need a medic," she said, hoping that none of his men were medics. "It could be a bacterial." Bacterial bullets were illegal throughout the Pact, but it was known that there were always a certain number of them around.

"Bacterial?" the sergeant repeated, taking an involuntary step backward.

"Might be," she said. "Better not get too close."

"Bacterial. Holy bloody backfire. You need quarantine right away. There's a medic station back that way." He nodded his head in the direction he'd come from. "Sorry, soldier." The sergeant barked a few sharp words to his squad and they moved off briskly.

Jessine at last remembered where the lifts were, and headed directly for them.

She reached them without meeting anyone else. You could tell today was special — the Palace was usually bustling with people, humans and aliens, doing the work of the Pact. Stepping into the freight cage, she pressed the code for Kitchley's floor. As the door closed, she leaned back against the wall and caught her breath. As the lift rose, it occurred to Jessine that anyone looking for her might think to check Kitchley's office. It was well known around the Palace that the High Secretary's Appointments Clerk and the High Secretary's new wife worked together. She punched the code for the High Secretary's Retreat, three floors below Kitchley's. She could take the stairs, and not be a sitting duck when the lift doors opened.

She stepped out into the domed chamber, looking up toward the white-and-gold balconies rising over her. The lavish Daphne ferns threw out their baroque tendrils along the spiraled trellis, their white and silver blossoms scenting the air with a curious mixture of saffron and honey. The one remaining Retreat of the original twelve, it had not yet surrendered to the space-hungry beast of bureaucracy. It still had the lush and elaborate grace that the High Secretary was supposed to enjoy. Standing here, among the plants, she could almost forget the battles outside.

The retreat, blue and silver with touches of rosy mauve, was awash with tranquility. It reminded her of Cowper Bouriere, who had been kind to her, and who had not pretended that an arranged marriage was a love match. For that alone, she *did* love him.

Jessine heard the discreet beep of an alarm, and somewhere beyond the retreat there was the sound of glastic breaking. Her grip on the Ridly tightened a fraction.

Shots crashed above her and the balustrade of one of the balconies shattered.

Jessine moved back, hiding in the rich curl of a huge Daphne fern.

Two minutes went interminably by. Jessine listened but heard nothing more than the continuing beep of the alarm. She couldn't wait here forever. She had to know if Kitchley had survived, and if she would be safe with him.

But the stairs were monitored, and open besides. She looked up the shaft of the ancient fern. It grew three stories, branching off with broad leaves and thick stems. Some of the heavier branches passed close by balconies. Holstering the Ridly in the waistband of her pants, she began to climb.

She climbed steadily, cautiously, taking care to examine each balcony thoroughly as it came into view.

For an instant she thought of Damien Ver, and was startled at how concerned she was for him. What was he doing? Why had he sent those men for her? Did he really just want her safe, or did he want the Secretariat? Near the top of the fern, Jessine stopped to rest and to re-evaluate her position. From here she could see that someone had used railguns on the elaborate ceiling, blasting away the mural of the Creation of the Pact in which all the great heroes sat together in front of a High Secretary who looked a bit like Jessine's husband.

"Oh, Cowper," she whispered. "You didn't deserve this. You weren't a bad man." She stared at the painting, fighting back unexpected tears. Did she have any chance at all? Did any of them?

Peering through the foliage, ears straining, Jessine tried to determine if the area was clear. It seemed so, and she crawled out along a branch to the nearest balcony.

Then she heard a voice from a window above her and froze.

"Step out," came the sharp order from a Security sergeant, his railgun ready for business.

Jessine straightened up. She recognized him. "Good afternoon, Sergeant Mallas," she said distinctly, glad that her voice did not shake.

"Madame Bouriere," said Sergeant Mallas, hurriedly lowering his railgun and flushing with embarrassment. "I didn't realize . . . And your arm. Do you need medical attention?" He was two balconies away, but appeared to be considering climbing over the railings and balustrades in order to reach her.

"Step out into the hall," suggested Jessine, starting there herself.

"No," said Sergeant Mallas, showing his anxiety again. "It isn't safe. Stay where you are. I'll come and escort you."

She faltered, then made herself nod in approval. "That would be very welcome. Thank you, Sergeant." She made an effort to straighten her clothing and her hair while the young soldier made his way around to her balcony.

"We were all so worried," the sergeant said as he came to her side. "No one knows what . . . excuse me, Madame Bouriere." He dropped to one knee and fired his railgun at a shadow in the hall. The pellets spattered and the shadow retreated.

"Who . . . ?" Jessine asked.

"Who knows? Cernians, Navy, Treasury, Marines, Kona Tatsu?" He made a face to show it was all the same to him. "They're all out fighting with us. Nobody knows who's alive and who's not, or who's in charge." He coughed. "I didn't mean to say anything wrong, Madame Bouriere."

"Saying it isn't wrong, Sergeant Mallas. It's the act of rebellion that's wrong." She indicated the hallway. "I want to reach Kitchley's office. That's one more level above us."

The Sergeant shook his head. "I don't know, Madame. It could be pretty hard getting through the halls. There are too many people who . . . don't know what's going on. They're barricaded in their offices and shooting at anything moving." He looked at her pistol. "Still, considering —"

Jessine cocked her head. "You mean considering that most of them would recognize me —"

He nodded. "It's taking a chance. Most of them think you and all the others are dead."

"I can understand why," said Jessine, and could not keep herself from adding, "Do you know if anyone else . . . ?"

"Got out?" he finished for her. "Sorry, Madame. I don't know. I've heard rumors, but nothing real." He pressed closer to the open door. "You want to try this?"

"Yes," she said, knowing it was what she had to do. She had been raised to be the wife of the High Secretary, and that included facing adversity with dignity and fortitude. She stood a little straighter. "Take up First Escort position."

"If that's what you want," said Sergeant Mallas dubiously but without challenging her orders. He moved into the hall.

"Stand up, Sergeant. They are less likely to fire at you if you behave as if you belong here."

The first checkpoint was unmanned, but the

second had Security soldiers in place, all four of them heavily armed.

"You're cleared to the Appointments Directorate, Madame," said the unsmiling Security guard. "Treasury Guards are in charge there. You'll have to deal with them if you're going beyond there."

"Thank you, Monitor," said Jessine with deliberate hauteur; she had the satisfaction of seeing the Security guards come to attention before she followed Sergeant Mallas through the confusion of the main corridor.

The five make-shift data processing stations which had been set up under the Grand Staircase more than twenty years ago were now filled with Directorate employees all trying to sort and destroy any compromising documents they might have in their records. Dataspools and printed records lay everywhere — on the floor, atop cases and chairs and cabinets — and everyone spoke in whispers, as if they, too, might prove embarrassing to some high official.

Sergeant Mallas kept his eyes moving, watching for the unexpected as he continued at a steady walk toward the next checkpoint.

A cluster of offices toward the first bank of dropshafts had once been storage rooms; they were small and cramped and dark. Clerks were assigned to them on a rotating basis because few could stand the sepulchral environment for long. Sergeant Mallas was starting to say something when the door to the nearest office was flung open and half a dozen soldiers in Navy body-armor uniforms piled out, their Kanovskys at the ready.

Jessine did not want to find out what kind of ammunition the Kanovskys had. Sergeant Mallas tugged her off her feet and dropped almost on top of her, his gun aimed at the Navy soldiers.

"We can kill you and take her or take her," said the leader of the Navy soldiers, making a suggestive flick with the barrel of his Kanovsky. "Get out of the way, Security. This isn't your fight anymore."

"Whose fight is it?" Jessine demanded, half her body feeling squashed. Her cheek was pressed against the floor and her hip bone hurt.

"Be quiet, Madame," Sergeant Mallas said to her, remaining very calm.

"Let us have her," the Navy leader said. "You can go. We don't want you."

I'm going to die here, thought Jessine with intense disbelief. *They are going to kill Sergeant Mallas and me. I'm twenty-four. They can't do this.* She bit the insides of her cheeks to keep from screaming in rage.

Sergeant Mallas pressed his release toggle. "I'm ready any time you are."

"It's a damned waste," sighed the leader, and brought his Kanovsky up.

He never fired it. A group of Treasury Guards stepped out of the dropshaft, their weapons — Bahkoyn 149JZs — already aimed. The TechCaptain in the lead made a motion and his men spread out across the wide section of corridor in front of the dropshafts.

"Holy sweet —" whispered Sergeant Mallas, looking from the Navy soldiers to the Treasury detachment.

Jessine ground her teeth. Either they were going to kill her, in which case she wanted them to get it over with, or they were going to fight each other, in which case she wanted to be on her way. She pushed one arm out from under her and tried to shove herself free of Sergeant Mallas, who moved at once to continue to cover her.

"Madame Bouriere," said the TechCaptain. "Can we be of service?"

The Navy soldiers were now maneuvering into position to fight the guards. The Kanovskys faced the Bahkoyns; no one fired yet.

"I want to get to Kitchley."

"He's injured, Madame Bouriere," said the

TechCaptain, as polite as if they were preparing for a diplomatic reception. "But he is in his office." He gave his attention to the Navy soldiers. "We'll take it from here."

"Uh-oh," whispered Sergeant Mallas, and started to slide backward, dragging Jessine with him.

It was difficult to tell who had fired first: there was silence, and then the hallway rang and buzzed with Kanovsky full-deterrent ammunition and Bahkoyn high impact shells. The ornamental friezes above the dropshafts splintered and shells gouged long grooves in the floor.

Four Navy soldiers dropped at the first onslaught, three dead and one wounded. Treasury guards' repellent-field uniforms managed better, though two men were wounded.

The firing increased and there were screams and howls everywhere, from Navy soldiers, Treasury Guards, clerks, automatic alarm systems. The noise was as frightening as the shells being fired.

"We're getting out of here," Sergeant Mallas told Jessine, wriggling back and sideways from the firefight.

The Treasury troops moved toward the Navy unit, clearly holding the advantage. The Navy soldiers retreated back toward the tomb-like cubicle offices, taking more time to aim and fire than they had done at first. Behind them at the far end of the hall clerks were screaming and running, many with their arms full of dataspools.

Sergeant Mallas inched his way closer to the dropshafts. "Just one floor up," he reminded Jessine. "You can do it easy. You slide back, stand up real carefully — you don't want to pinwheel."

"What about you?" she asked as she did her best to follow his instructions.

"I'm right behind you." He kept his railgun in position to fire, watching the guards drive the Navy out of the hall.

Jessine slipped into the dropshaft, steadying herself in the field, taking care to stay balanced and oriented properly. A bullet ricocheted off the floor and struck Sergeant Mallas square in the chest just as he was easing back into the dropshaft. He gave a single grunt, then his rail-gun dropped from his fingers. He fell sideways, slipping beyond the field's stability; his corpse began to turn slowly, then moved steadily faster in the dropshaft beside Jessine as she rose to the floor above. She heard shots behind her, but didn't dare look back as she stepped out. Probably some other faction was attacking the Navy — Sclerida's men.

Jessine jogged along the corridor and swung

around a corner into the Appointments Communications Center. It had been transformed into a command post for the defense of the Secretary's Palace and was as crowded as the corridor had been. Stopped, she saw that five railguns were aimed at her. Only the sudden shouts of two alien supervisors stopped the clerks manning the guns from firing.

A Magdarite with orange ruff fully extended around his vulpine face, rushed forward, bowing in recognition. "Madame Bouriere. How . . . fortunate to see you." He seemed confused but determined to behave correctly no matter how strange their circumstances.

Jessine took this as well as she could, but she felt at a marked disadvantage. "I don't know what's . . . developed. It's been so — " She stopped, gesturing her lack of words.

"Untypical," the Magdarite supplied, doing his best to look calm. "We're getting the situation in hand now, as you can see." He bowed to the soldiers and clerks. "It is a great honor to defend you in this difficult hour."

"It is an honor to be defended by you." Jessine nodded regally. "Can I get on the other side of these guns now?"

Finally, he led her around the railguns and past a barricade of office furniture. A little giddily, Jessine wondered if double-decker desks were the daily operating standard. "You'll want to see Kitchley," assumed the Magdarite.

"Yes, please."

"Right this way, Madame Bouriere," the Magdarite said as he started through a maze of cubicles.

"Is Kitchley well?" asked Jessine.

"A little injured, but not severely," said the Magdarite, letting his ruff deflate a little. "He has been tended to, and should recover completely." They were nearing Kitchley's office, and Jessine saw two communication-dispatchers now set up as gun emplacements with impressive bits of artillery wired into them. "We are striving to give thorough protection here."

"Yes, it looks it," said Jessine, her face set in the ritual half-smile she habitually wore at public functions. She inclined her head to the clerks who recognized her.

"His Remarkableness the Appointment Clerk to the High Secretary," said the Magdarite, with a court bow.

Kitchley was preoccupied with the displays on the huge wall screen, and so at first did not realize who had come into his large, cramped office. When he at last he turned, a great smile wreathed his face. "Madame Bouriere," he said warmly.

"Kitchley," she said, a little surprised at the relief she felt. She maintained a decent fortitude and merely grasped his wrists as custom dictated. "I was afraid that you'd been harmed when — "

Kitchley shook his head. "They ignored me. They really wanted you. I thought we'd lost you. Come, sit, please. Do you need a medic?" He gestured at her bloody arm.

"No, thank you," said Jessine politely. She looked around the cramped office area and found a large sealed crate. Carefully removing a stack of papers, she sat down.

Kitchley was at his comm board. "Team X, this is Leader. The subject has returned safely. Please pick up soonest."

"Team X, will comply. ETA, five minutes," came the answer.

Jessine stared at Kitchley for a second. "Oh. Your escort."

Kitchley gave her a reassuring smile. "Yes, Madame. They'll be here shortly, and we can carry on getting you safely to my house." His smile disappeared. "We have the preliminary report on the autopsy."

The word gave the High Secretary's death a reality that Jessine had been holding off. Tears filled her eyes. "Yes?"

"It appears he was poisoned. We are proceeding on the assumption that the assassination may well have been at the instigation of Senator Lomax. He has made it plain enough that he covets the post of High Secretary and is prepared to take steps to secure the position for himself. Therefore it is not unlikely that he participated in these dreadful events." He watched the display critically: nine levels below, Cernians and Navy soldiers were locked in combat.

"Why Lomax and not Sclerida?" asked Jessine. She wiped her forehead with the back of her hand. She thought she remembered having this discussion before with Kitchley. She wondered if he knew something she didn't. "Sclerida's every bit as ambitious as Lomax and he has half the Navy at his command."

"Yes, the Admiral is another likely candidate, but Lomax seems to have gained the most in the least time." He pressed one of his fingers to the center of his forehead, the Daphne equivalent to a frown. "Of course, it's too soon to be sure. We don't know what the disposition will be a day from now."

Jessine stared at the display. "No, we don't."

"If it is Lomax," said Kitchley, "then he will have to shore up his claim quickly. That would require that he ally himself with you or your step-daughter."

"You mean marry me or Tira," said Jessine more bluntly. "A statement of endorsement wouldn't be enough for him." A shudder of distaste rippled through her. "He would need something more . . . binding."

In the momentary lull of their conversation, the voice of a soldier could be heard: "Unit 44, to 6 North, unit 44, go to 6 North. Reinforce against Cernian invaders."

"Unit 44, roger, wilco."

Kitchley regarded Jessine. "Yes, marriage, to you or Tira." He hesitated. "Or he could dispose of Wiley and claim his position. And then there is the Haiken Maru. They have influence enough to make the lad a puppet; Wiley is not prepared to resist such pressures."

Dispose of? Jessine looked sharply at Kitchley. Had Cowper's death caused this callousness, or had it always been there?

"I'm afraid you're right," she said slowly. "Even if he were popular, he isn't very strong-willed." She reviewed what she knew of her husband's wild son. He was popular, sometimes even quite charming, but his cronies took joy in antagonizing the alien population. He just hadn't exhibited very good judgment. "He couldn't hold the Secretariat on his own." She looked at the display. "Where is Wiley? Have you found him?"

81

"No, we haven't," admitted Kitchley, his embarrassment obvious. "We are assuming that is an indication he is still alive, somewhere."

"Will they keep looking for him?" asked Jessine as they moved.

"Of course," replied Kitchley. "He *is* the heir."

"Lomax or Sclerida, there isn't much to choose between them for Wiley," said Jessine slowly.

"I fear not," said Kitchley. "I haven't located Admiral Sclerida, either. A man of his great abilities —"

"And ruthlessness," added Jessine.

"Yes, ruthlessness, certainly," said Kitchley. "Sclerida may lack Senatorial status, but he had the good sense to marry a Chaney, which improves his lot and makes his children serious candidates for the High Secretariat." He tapped his fingers on the armrest. "Despite the scandal his children might well be his access to the office he seeks. With Chaney prestige — his brother-in-law still supports him — who knows what he might achieve."

Jessine nodded. "He's been putting pressure on the High Secretary for some time now, wanting to arrange a marriage between his son Dov and Tira. It would be perfect for his plans. Cowper and I discussed it . . ." Her voice trailed off. Cowper had wanted her perspective since she was so close to Tira's age. Jessine tried to remember if she'd really considered Tira's feelings during those talks.

"I'm going to miss him," she said to Kitchley. "He was a very decent man. He treated me well and he did his job the best he knew how."

"I had great esteem for him," said Kitchley. For the next several seconds he concentrated on a pitched confrontation in the lower storage depths. A group of Marines was attempting to cart off large canisters of some unknown substance while Treasury soldiers pinned them down. "If the Admiral should ever persuade Tira to marry Dov Sclerida, it could lead to a number of unpleasant developments."

"There we agree," said Jessine with feeling. "But I doubt Tira would see it that way." She pointed out the North Reception lobby monitor, which showed a disordered group of Security soldiers had just broken through a Cernian barricade.

Kitchley used his palace communications over-ride to warn all the combatants that if they did not evacuate the area, explosives concealed in the floor would be triggered, killing all in the lobby. As he watched the soldiers scatter in all directions, he said, "There is no change of heart there."

"No," said Jessine heavily. "She still calls me

harlot. She refuses to believe that her father isn't
. . . wasn't jealous, that our marriage was a diplomatic convenience. And once she found out
about Damien Ver, well . . ."

"She's not a foolish girl generally," said
Kitchley, doing his best to be reassuring. "In time
she will come to understand —"

"I doubt it," said Jessine, feeling strangely
desolate. "Given what has happened. Her father
is a martyr, and I'm sure Tira assumes I was the
one who betrayed him."

Kitchley's attention returned to the monitors.
As he had warned, he picked up a small trigger
unit and pressed it into action: on the display one
of the holograms showed an eruption of stone
and glastic as a dozen uniformed bodies were
hurled from the landing arms outside the
Ambassadorial entrance.

"Good!" Jessine approved as she watched the
display.

"Necessary," corrected Kitchley. "If I were not
loyal to the Pact, I would not be able to send
men to their deaths in this way. We must have a
true succession, or the Pact will become mean-
ingless, and everything that we have struggled so
hard to achieve will be lost."

Jessine regarded him in surprise. "I didn't . . .
you've never said you were a . . . a patriot before."

"Because I am an alien, you expect me to despise the Pact? Why? Before the Pact there were more abuses and they were worse. With the Pact there is a little hope that the time will come when the abuses will end. For that I am willing to do battle." He stopped suddenly. "That is why I am determined to do everything in my power to protect the succession."

Jessine tilted her seat back, stared at the ceiling a moment before closing her eyes.

"None of us could hold the Secretariat," she said. "Not Wiley, not me, not Tira. And yet any one of us could take it for one of these mad factions."

"It's Wiley's seat, Madame. We must find a way for him to hold it. Perhaps the Kona Tatsu . . ."

Jessine gave him a look. "We must *find* him first. And the Kona Tatsu . . . I don't know anymore what the Kona Tatsu wants." She squeezed her eyes tight. Was it the Kona Tatsu or Damien Ver who had sent those APC's? Or had Varrick lied and it was someone else altogether?

"Let me be certain I have the players straight," said Jessine. "The Haiken Maru want Lomax in the seat, as Wiley's puppeteer — maybe his regent. Sclerida wants the seat for himself, but hasn't got a prayer for that, or of becoming regent, not after that scandal — did he really think his wife would let his boyfriends live in *her house*?

"So Sclerida would need to . . . dispose . . . of Wiley and marry Dov to me or Tira. Blech." Jessine didn't like young Sclerida — he was shallow, egotistical and stupid to boot.

"You could be regent for Wiley, Madame," offered Kitchley. "And Sclerida could marry you to Dov and gain the seat that way."

"No, he *couldn't* marry me to Dov," she snapped. "I wouldn't marry Dov Sclerida."

Kitchley protested. "But, Madame, to protect the succession . . ."

"The succession cannot be protected, Kitchley," said Jessine sharply. "Wiley is not fit to rule, regardless of regent or advisors. If he takes the Secretariat, the Pact will take another step down towards death."

"If he doesn't, the Pact will die immediately," shot back Kitchley.

"Then we're doomed, aren't we?" Jessine leaned her seat back again. "Because I don't think that Sclerida *or* Lomax could run the Pact for anything but their own benefit."

They were both silent for a moment.

"There *is* Governor Merikur."

"Who?" asked Jessine.

"The governor of Harmony Cluster," replied

Kitchley. "Well, governor pro tem. He was *Admiral* Merikur until the Kona Tatsu assassinated Governor Windsor. I believe he's on his way to Earth, with a fleet of cluster command ships."

"Oh, splendid," muttered Jessine. "Another hand in the pot. And who does Governor Merikur intend to marry? Me, Tira or Wiley?"

"I'm not sure he knows that the High Secretary is dead," replied Kitchley thoughtfully. "He's been en route for a few weeks now."

Jessine's eyes narrowed. "What's he after then?"

Kitchley raised his eyebrow. "With a cluster command fleet? I understand he's already taken over Apex Cluster."

"Rebellion? *Before* the Secretary died? How ambitious!"

"Begun by Governor Windsor, Madame. That would be why the Kona Tatsu killed him."

"How curious," murmured Jessine. "A man without a corporation. I mean, Lomax is run by the Haiken Maru, and Sclerida has Naval Logistics . . . what did Windsor have? Or who had him?"

Jessine moved restlessly through the crowded room toward Kitchley's displays. "The way you handle things, I have to be glad we're on the same side. You're an expert tactician."

"Oh, no," said Kitchley with modesty. "It would not be a life for me, fighting and plotting. I will do what is necessary to protect the Pact, but I could not make a career out of aggression. You will find that many of the aliens working here feel as I do." He paused, watching the fire from a Kanovsky 40-09 tear the hell out of one of the statues outside the Ambassadorial reception salons. "I will be grateful when this is over. It is not a thing I relish."

"No, of course you don't," said Jessine at once. "I wonder when we'll get a report on Wiley's whereabouts."

"I don't know," said Kitchley. "When things are a bit calmer, I will press my inquiries."

"And Tira?" As always, Jessine had a complex reaction to her step-daughter. "Do you know where she is? In spite of everything, I hope she's all right."

"We haven't found her anywhere in the Palace," Kitchley said. "She must have escaped."

"To where?" asked Jessine hopelessly. "With whom?"

"I don't know," Kitchley confessed. "We haven't a full picture of what is happening within the Palace, let alone anywhere else. I cannot tell you, not even with these display screens, who exactly is defending the Palace or whether the defenders are losing. It will take time before we know the whole of the damage here."

"How long do you expect that will take?" Jessine asked.

"It depends," Kitchley said. "If there are more waves of assault, it will take a great deal of time. If there are no more waves of assault, then we must determine which group has been able to secure what area, and only then will we have some notion of who is losing and who is winning."

Knowing it showed more weakness than she wanted to admit, Jessine asked one more question. "And Damien Ver?"

Kitchley made a gesture of apology. "He is wearing his blank. We can't find him unless he removes it."

"Or unless he dies," said Jessine. "We're not winning, are we?" she asked as she stared at the displays in Kitchley's make-shift headquarters.

"Not yet," said Kitchley. "But neither are we losing."

"Not yet," amended Jessine.

Kitchley turned to Jessine, his slanted tiger's eyes sharp. "Before the escort arrives, I must ask you an impolite question."

"Yes?" Jessine said.

"Where does Damien Ver stand in this? Have

you made him promises?" The last was said gently but it was still an accusation.

Jessine colored. "Not the kind you're implying," she told him in sudden anger. "He has never said or done anything that led me to believe that he had other ambitions."

"I ask because," Kitchley persisted, "it would be possible for him to find a husband for you, one of excellent birth who would be willing to let Ver rule through him, one who would accept the same terms that Cowper Bouriere did in his marriage to you, and that would serve his purpose very well. He is used to working out of sight. With your support, Ver would be able to lead the Pact."

"It's not like that," said Jessine, denying her own doubts. One of the reasons she was so attracted to Ver was that he was a man of purpose and determination: but what if his determination was greater than he had admitted to her?

"It is not that he is not capable," Kitchley said, "but it would not be accepted, not at this time. If the Governors were being more reasonable, I would advise just such an arrangement, but in these times, more visible solutions are necessary."

This was more than she could handle. "How

can you say this to me?" Jessine demanded. "You know me, Kitchley. You and I have been friends. I *trust* you."

"And I you, but if there are questions, I must be prepared to answer them," Kitchley said reasonably. He gave Jessine one last, long stare. "You are telling me the truth, aren't you? This isn't the work of the Kona Tatsu and Damien Ver?"

"If it is, he has betrayed all of us." She said it coldly, but it struck the deeper and more painfully for that.

There was a disturbance outside the barrier and the Magdarite bustled into Kitchley's space.

"The escort has arrived, Your Remarkableness."

"Excellent." Kitchley gestured Jessine to leave the cubicle before him. They passed the railgun emplacements and joined a squad of well-armed Daphneans. They hurried through the corridors to the staircase, heading for the roof.

Jessine frowned at Kitchley. "Is there a communication center at your compound in Horizon Park?"

"Of course, and a staff to tend to it. You will not be cut off from the world just because you are protected." He put his long, narrow hand on her shoulder again. "Rest assured, you will be all right."

"Thank you," she said.

Kitchley indicated the aircar. "Come. I have done everything I can here. We must continue our efforts at Horizon Park."

"Then we will," said Ereley, the leader of the escort, starting toward the aircar where the other Daphneans waited.

Kitchley hesitated. "I will be with you directly. Climb aboard, Ereley. There's a message I have to send to your friend, Madame, if he can receive it. He will want to know where you are."

"Yes, Madame," said Ereley. "Let me help you get aboard."

"All right," said Jessine, glancing back toward Kitchley. "Hurry up."

"Of course, Madame," came the muffled reply.

Ereley was aboard and the aircar throbbed into life. He looked around at the men with him, then nodded to the driver. "We're ready."

Jessine, who was just buckling herself into the harness, stared over at him. "Wait! I see Kitchley coming."

"So he is," said Ereley. And with that, he swung his Kanovsky around and blasted Kitchley with a burst of metal-piercing shots. Kitchley staggered, then appeared to drop into pieces, his lower body almost entirely severed from the upper. Bright orange Daphnean blood fountained into the consoles and communications equipment.

If it had been possible Jessine would have risen. But the harness held her down and the aircar was already starting to move through the concealed port, the sounds of its engines covering her rising scream.

Chapter 6

They dropped out of the night like wounded owls and jolted into the ground. Wiley, more dazed than Nika, fell flat on his back. The world was wobbling. It was different from his usual post-party wobble, and he didn't like it. Especially since the post had cut the party so short.

"We've got to get out of here," Nika said as she

gathered the chute together and looked around for a place to hide it.

"I like it here," mumbled Wiley. "It's so . . . so . . . it's *flat*. It's not *moving*." His head ached, his back ached, his ankles ached. In fact, there was no part of him that wasn't sore in some way. He groaned as he sat up. "So what's going on, anyway?"

"It's complicated," she said. "We have to get out of here. They could be looking for us."

Wiley sighed as he stared at the empty street. "All right. Where do we go now?"

"We need transportation. Look around for something that has good speed and handling. I don't want to blunder around up there." She stretched a little, then regarded him with exaggerated patience. "Well? Do you think you can manage to get up now?"

Wiley pushed himself to his feet. He felt slightly dizzy. Functional, though, if someone else did the thinking.

"You look awful," said Nika. "Let's get going. We need an aircar, now."

Wiley shrugged and fell in beside her, though it was an effort to match her long, steady stride. "If that's what you want, that's what we'll do."

She glanced at him. "You're going to have to learn to be more assertive than that if you intend to run the Pact."

They had gone some distance when Wiley spotted a Kahna Starcruiser. It was driven by a stern-faced man with military bearing whose passenger was a Zambretic merchant in full regalia.

"Pretty. Should I stick out my thumb?" Wiley asked. Nika murmured something he couldn't hear.

In a moment, the Starcruiser had come to a halt before them. The chauffeur was punching uselessly at his controls and his passenger was blue with indignation.

Nika stepped up to the car as the door opened. "Out," she said. The chauffeur looked at her, then at his passenger. A weapon appeared in the woman's hand. "Now," she added. The chauffeur rose from his seat. The merchant began to bluster. Nika raised her weapon hand and Wiley stepped forward hastily.

"Please," he said. "I realize this is a great inconvenience, but there has been an emergency, and I am required at the Palace at once. I regret that we must deprive you of the aircar, but you may reclaim it at the Palace in the next twenty-four hours. You will be compensated for our use and any disadvantage this causes you."

The chauffeur clearly recognized Wiley. He turned to the owner of the aircar. "He's right, sir.

We must cooperate. But you will be rewarded for your service."

"We do not permit such abuses on Zambra," said the merchant. He got down from the aircar in a huff and refused to be impressed by the diplomatic thanks Wiley extended to him before climbing into the Starcruiser.

"So what official business are we on, anyway? Who *are* you?" Wiley's head hurt.

"At the moment, I'm your bodyguard. Strap in."

Wiley strapped in. "Where are we going now?"

"Somewhere you'll be safe."

They were headed out of the city again. Looking for her precious drop point, Wiley assumed. He was beginning to have suspicions about this woman.

After several minutes, they approached a group of buildings. A little shanty town, Wiley saw, built around a factory. Nika landed the aircar in one of the narrow streets. As she hustled him out the starboard hatch, two men slid in the port side.

"Valet parking," commented Wiley, looking back over his shoulder. "Very nice."

Nika tugged on his arm. She led Wiley toward one of the tumbledown shops. NORF'S BAR AND GRILL, read the sign. "Oh, good," said Wiley. "I was starting to get the munchies."

The hostess approached them on tiny cloven hooves. Her slim legs disappeared up under a tight skirt. "Dinner or drinks?" she asked.

"Both," replied Wiley.

"We're meeting someone," added Nika. "A party of six; the name is Jones."

"Right this way, please." Wiley watched the hostess as she led them toward the back. Maybe if he hadn't blown off so many boring political dinners, he'd know what species she was.

She showed them to a small private dining room. The table was indeed set for six, but no one else was in the room. When the hostess had shut the door behind them, Nika went to the far wall, muttering under her breath.

"Come on, Wiley," she called.

"What about dinner?" he demanded. "I'm hungry."

A section of wall slid aside.

"Later. We have to keep moving."

Wiley shook his head and followed her. Would the surprises never end?

They stepped into a dropshaft, the wall closing as they fell.

Falling through the dim light of the dropshaft, Wiley tried to count the floors. Not a chance. A long way, he could figure that much out.

Then Nika grabbed him and they stopped,

stepping out to a security station. Behind two panels of glastic, underneath cameras and guns, sat a live human guard. Wiley thought he recognized the black uniform.

"You're Kona Tatsu," he whispered.

Nika stepped up to the comm panel and pressed her hand against the ID plate. "Yes." She stepped aside and gestured for Wiley to use the panel.

He put his hand up to the plate, then turned to look into her face. "Why?" he asked. "What's happened?"

A door opened, letting them into the space between the glastic panels. The second door opened only after the first had shut again. Nika pushed at Wiley.

"The High Secretary is dead," she said. "The Secretarial Palace is under attack by a number of groups." She led him down a corridor as she talked. "We hope to be able to keep you safe here, for a while, at least. If we have to, we'll keep moving you around until it's over."

Wiley nodded. He felt terrible. He'd had too much to drink, too much . . . excitement, certainly too much falling, and still hadn't had dinner.

"I don't guess there's been a mistake about my father," he said.

"No," said Nika. "No mistake." She looked at him. "I'm sorry."

Wiley looked away from her. He wasn't sure if he was going to cry, but if he was, he didn't want to do it in front of the Kona Tatsu. Not live agents, anyhow, he amended, thinking of the security cameras that must be around.

"Come on, let's get you that dinner," said Nika.

They moved through several corridors, turning corners until Wiley was sure they were no longer under the tavern. Finally, they entered a dining room. Wiley was a little startled to see the tablecloths and human waiters.

"Where *are* we?"

"Welcome to the gracious Kona Tatsu Café," said a waiter, leading them to a table.

"Two specials, Jack," said Nika. "Getting shot at makes me hungry."

"Everything makes you hungry," said Jack. "Food'll be right out." He disappeared behind a folding screen.

Wiley leaned back in his chair. "So you're Kona Tatsu."

Nika smiled. "Yup. And you're the heir to the Secretariat."

Wiley drooped. "Thanks."

Nika's smile vanished. "Wiley, you can't hide. Not from Sclerida, not from Haiken Maru, and certainly not from the Secretariat."

"Then what's this for?" Wiley gestured around him.

"The time being," replied Nika. "It's temporary. Until things settle a little, and we can talk instead of shoot."

"Then I'll have to grow up. Take the damn chair, pick up the reins."

"You don't want to."

"A prize for the lady in shreds," said Wiley. Nika gave her rumpled clothing a quick glance, then shrugged.

"No," Wiley continued. "I don't. I don't understand how any of it works, regardless of how much attention I pay. *And* I don't much want to be someone's puppet, so it doesn't matter that I'd have a regent."

"Is that why you party all the time?" asked Nika.

Wiley threw up his hands. "What else am I going to do? What am I actually good for?"

Jack appeared beside their table. "The food will be —"

"Haiken Maru!"

Nika and Jack turned; Wiley stared. An injured man had stumbled into the dining room.

"The safe house is under attack," he said. "Haiken Maru forces are spreading like ants. Better get him out of here." He waved at Wiley.

Nika stood. "Right. Let's go."

Wiley shoved his chair back. "So much for bodily sustenance."

"Through the kitchen," ordered Jack. "Up the tube, aircar on the roof." He pulled a weapon and headed for the door. Nika grabbed Wiley's arm and pulled. He followed, running.

In the kitchen was indeed a lift tube. They jumped in. As they shot past the first few floors, they could hear sirens and yelling.

Nika took off her belt. "Put this on." She reached around Wiley and fastened the belt for him. "It's got my AID. It'll take care of you."

"But you'll be here," protested Wiley.

"Maybe not," she shot back. "We didn't expect them to find you here." She pulled two weapons from some fold in her battered garment as they neared the roof.

"Look, thanks for . . . your help," offered Wiley. "Even if . . ."

Nika looked him in the eyes. "Sorry about dinner."

The tube stopped them and she stepped out, both guns blazing. Wiley had a momentary flash: what if there were Kona Tatsu on the roof?

But there weren't, only Cernians, and Nika was cut down before him like a paper doll in a shredder.

"But . . ." Wiley fell to his knees beside her and was jerked to his feet.

"Come with us," barked the Cernian. He pulled Wiley toward a waiting APC.

"Of course." Wiley wasn't hungry anymore.

Chapter 7

Chaney and Tira stood breathless, listening. The guards were on the floor, bound and gagged. Chaney stared at Uncle Ken's body.

"I don't understand," he said. "Why? What did he want?"

Tira watched him. His puzzlement made her think: he really *didn't* understand. He'd thought his uncle was trustworthy. Loyal.

But to whom? Tira bit her lip reflectively. She was beginning to trust Yon Chaney, maybe even to like him a bit.

"We can't stay," she said gently. "Where do we go from here?"

"Not out the way we came in, that's certain," said Chaney. "There are armed guards, and if that tunnel isn't mined, I'm a Lakme swamp-devil. We can't get out that way, even if we could get transportation."

"So what do we do, then?" Tira asked. "We can't wait here for them to find us."

"No, of course not." He looked around. "Uncle Ken came from that direction. The chances are there aren't as many guards that way. It's supposed to be protected on this side, so let's go that way. It's probably safer." He claimed another pistol, giving him a total of three.

He led Tira to the far door.

They were lucky; no guards were posted in the back hallway at all.

As they walked through the corridors, it became clear that they'd left the working installation and were now in a residence. An elaborate private residence, fitted with brocade drapes and tile floors. Along the walls were portraits of famous admirals of the past. One showed Secretary Bouriere and Admiral Sclerida reviewing a fine display of Naval aerobatic aircars and pursuit boats.

"Where are we?" whispered Tira.

"The official answer is 'Naval Logistics Headquarters.' What it really is is Admiral Sclerida's private palace," Chaney answered. The corridor was still empty as he tried the nearest door, one with elaborate carvings over the lintel.

It gave onto an opulent suite of three rooms, each an astonishing realization of a fantasy. In the first there were more lush tropical plants than Chaney had seen outside of the Secretarial arboretum. Two streams wound through the large room, and brightly colored birds called from the dense foliage. There was a scent of jungle flowers so sweet it was cloying. In the center of this all was a bed draped in gauzy fabric and made up with silkeen sheets. One wall concealed a closet, empty but for plant food.

"I don't like the feel of this," said Tira.

Chaney was silent. They moved on through the suite.

The second room was done up in rose-colored plush, containing three divans and two enormous hassocks. Overhead, the ceiling was draped in cinnamon-colored damask so that it appeared to be a tent instead of a room. Brass trays leaned against the wall and the smell of sandalwood was everywhere, rising up in fragrant smoke in braziers. A fountain perfumed the air with the scent of roses and jasmine. It hurt to breathe.

"No wonder there are aliens and humans who feel left out, who think they're taken advantage of. This place would convince them completely." Chaney scowled at the extravagance. "That fabric is off-planet hand-woven, and you won't get me to believe that the weavers are paid decently. The staff here is probably mostly aliens who answer to a few human supervisors, just like at any rich human's house. And the aliens probably live in shacks or tiny apartments with five pieces of furniture and a cooker."

"It makes you angry," said Tira.

"It makes me furious. Governor Windsor is right. The Pact isn't going to work until all the races are equal and all the planets are represented. If humans keep lording it over everyone else, the Pact will collapse and we'll be back to wars again." His eyes held an anger that surprised Tira.

"It's been this way for a long time, Yon," she said softly. "We're still here."

"Just barely. The Pact isn't thriving, it's getting by. That isn't good enough. The aliens are going to get less and less as the humans want more and more. No alliance can survive that. We need equality. Only then can the Pact prosper and thrive." He stopped suddenly. "Sorry. I didn't plan to —"

Several floors above them an alarm shrilled.

"What do you think?" Tira whispered, moving closer to Chaney. "Is it us?"

He listened. "No. It has nothing to do with us. That's a landing warning, I think. Something very large is coming in."

The third room was white-and-gilt, with statues of frolicking cherubs. There was a plethora of mirrors, all in elaborate gilt frames. And there was a tremendous bed occupying most of the far end of the room, its canopy supported by twisted pillars and topped with a golden crown.

"Come on, let's get moving," Tira said nervously.

"We've got to at least try to disguise you." Chaney looked around the room again, something unreadable in his eyes. Then he noticed a closet discreetly hidden behind a cavorting satyr. He rummaged through the clothing there. "Try these." He handed her a pair of flamboyant red pants. She held them up against her body.

"Are you serious? I'll look like a flare!"

"Put them on," ordered Chaney. "If they're looking at the pants, they won't see *you*.

Besides," he added, a little bitterly, "who ever looks at a fancy boy's face anyhow?"

Tira gave him a sharp look. "Fancy boy?"

Chaney handed her a black blouse and red vest. "Sclerida doesn't keep these clothes for himself."

"Then . . ."

"Just get dressed."

Tira ducked into the dressing alcove and changed quickly. Her leggings were tight, and the short britches she wore above them were not much looser. There was a long red vest edged in embroidery which she wore over a matching black lace shirt with a wide full collar that concealed the rise of her breasts. The only pair of boots she could find that fit her were ankle-height and golden. The pants had no pockets, but she was able to tuck her reticule into a blousy sleeve and one more weapon, retrieved from the guards, into her waistband, under the vest. She stuffed her own clothes into a hamper shaped like an urn and stepped back into the room. "Will it work?"

"You'll have to tie your hair back and change your make-up, but I can't see why anyone would suspect. I won't let them get close enough to check anything important." He did his best to laugh, and she dutifully tried to copy him. "What do you think?"

"I think we'd better get the guns, and then get out of here." Chaney's nervousness had returned full force.

"All right," said Tira. "It would have been nice to have a bath," she said wistfully.

"And a good meal and someone to clean up after," appended Chaney. "Maybe when all this is over. In the meantime, do something about your hair and face so we can get out of here."

She nodded, picked up her reticule, then sought out one of the mirrors. "Make-up?" she inquired as she surveyed the vast array of daubs and powders before her.

"Fancyboys usually wear stylized cosmetics. Soft mouths, sloe eyes. Tira, surely you've seen the look at the Palace."

She nodded. "All right. I'll see what I can do." She cleaned her face, then selected four tints to use on her skin. She made her eyebrows straighter, her lashes longer, and her mouth rounder. "Is this what you had in mind?"

Chaney was unnerved at how boyish yet pretty she looked. He rocked back on his heels. "Perfect! No one will notice your face."

"Splendid," responded Tira wryly.

Chaney blushed. "Of course. I didn't mean . . ."

"Don't worry about it. I just wish you could see me when I haven't been running for my life all day and dressed in a *woman's* clothes," said Tira lightly as she moved toward the door.

"Uh . . . I guess we should look for an aircar. Remember," he added, "walk very close to me, and when there are others around, hold my hand."

She looked startled. "Is that what's expected?"

"Yes." Chaney joined Tira at the door. He opened it and went out into the hall as if he had every right to be there, signaling at once for Tira to come after him. "We're going to take the dropshaft up to ground level. Try not to stare. I'm sorry. I'm really not sure what to do anymore. I thought you'd be safe here."

"Me, too." She bit her lip.

They kept moving. Climbing two sets of marble stairs brought them to a small door that gave out directly onto the landing field.

"Someone's landing, someone very important," said Chaney. He drew Tira close to him, draping his arm over her shoulder. She let him. "You see the tower? They're doing flag displays."

"They did that for my father," said Tira softly.

"Don't think about that now," said Chaney. "You'll need to do it later, but not now."

She nodded and leaned her head against his shoulder. "I know it's going to catch up with me. I can feel it waiting to happen."

"Hang on a little longer," Chaney encouraged her. "It's hard when you lose your father. I know."

"You lost yours?" she asked.

"Yeah. I lost him." His voice went sharp, then softened again. "When this is over, there'll be time. I . . . I'll be there. If you want."

She looked up at him. "I want, I think."

Kissing her was not part of his strategy, but it was suddenly the only thing worth doing. As he wrapped his arms around her, he felt the weapon tucked into her waistband at the small of her back. For some reason he could not identify, it made him hold her more tightly, and to deepen their kiss.

She gazed at him as he slowly released her.

He put one finger to her lips; his feelings were in such disorder that he could not speak. He made himself take her hand and walk a little further.

They looked out over the airfield. There were a dozen armed aircars hovering over its expanse. Electromagnetic defensive screens shimmered in the early morning light.

"Assault boats, three of them," said Chaney, pointing into the distance. "The lead has the Admiral's flashes on it." He took her hand again. "Let's go. If we can get to an aircar we can slip out when the Admiral's boat comes in."

As they came into the landing area, Tira asked, "What about the shields?"

"They're down for the landing. We have to get out before they close back up." He led the way through the corridor, not quite running. They rounded the first corner and found the first bay empty. "Keep going," he urged Tira as they rushed on.

In the second bay there was a military aircar, a Sprinter 377, ready and waiting.

"Get the hatch," Chaney told Tira. "And get in. Fast." He scanned the bay.

The door they'd just come through opened again, and a tall, old man flanked by two enormous Logistics guards stepped forward. He was resplendent in his full dress Admiral's uniform and he was smiling. "So you've come to see my triumphant departure." The smile widened. "Oh, yes, departure. You thought it was my arrival, didn't you?"

"Admiral Sclerida!" said Tira.

He bowed once. "It's been a long time, Demoiselle." He spoke languidly.

Chaney spun around, his weapon aimed directly at Admiral Sclerida, and knew he could not fire.

"Oh, come now. Don't spoil it, son." He came three steps nearer. "You've brought her to me, Yon."

Tira had opened the hatch, but hesitated, listening to the exchange.

"Get going," Chaney said over his shoulder. "Now."

She stepped into the aircar, but could not take her attention away from the guards.

"You can abandon these false heroics, Yon. You don't need to convince me, and it hardly matters what Demoiselle Bouriere thinks now. You've performed admirably." Admiral Sclerida beamed. "I knew you would show yourself my son, after all."

"Go!" bellowed Chaney, whirling to shove Tira into the aircar. "*GO!*" Tira did as he ordered, her mind still reeling with shock. Chaney turned back to his father, gun wavering.

Tira felt the aircar lift at a sharp angle, then had to wrestle with the controls to keep it stable as it rose into the morning. *Someone's shot out the buffers*, she thought. One of the Logistics guards must have fired on her. That had to be it. What else would cause the aircar to yaw the way it did?

Clinging to the skid beneath the aircar, Chaney watched the figure of his father shrink to a spot as the Sprinter climbed out of the defenses.

Chapter 8

Ereley knew the way to Horizon Park and he gave the driver concise instructions on the quickest way to reach the huge reserve. Like the others with him, he had donned a short vest with the spectrum painted on it, and wore an armband that said Rainbow Dawn.

Jessine sat very still, waiting to see what would

happen. She was still numbed by Kitchley's death, and at the hands of a fellow-Daphnean. More than anything she felt terribly tired.

As the aircar finally pulled away from the city, the Daphneans grew more relaxed, a few were almost jubilant. Sankley, who seemed to be second in command, began one of the traditional chants of the Daphneans, a steady, repetitious drone that the others joined, occasionally breaking out in high cawing sounds.

"You will admit it was a bold ploy, Madame," said Ereley as he took the empty place beside Jessine.

"What? Killing Kitchley?" She turned to him without fear. "He was helping you."

"Not he," said Ereley, contemptuous. "He was helping *you*. That was his only intent, to save you, human; he wouldn't have cared if all of us died in the process."

"He was my friend," said Jessine with feeling.

"He was your toady, you mean," said Ereley. "You liked him because he served you. If he had not done that, you wouldn't have paid any attention to him at all. You would have treated him like just another alien functionary."

Jessine did not answer at first, for she had to admit there was some truth in the accusation. "I knew him because he was the Appointments

Clerk," she said at last, very carefully. "I didn't have to like him for doing his job well. I liked him because he was a likeable man."

"Daphnean," corrected Ereley sharply. "He wasn't a human, he was Daphnean. We are all Daphnean here. Except you. You are the alien now." He could not conceal his satisfaction. When he smiled he gloated. "You will do what suits *us* best, for a change."

"What is it that suits you best?" she echoed, mistrusting even the sound of it.

The chanting was quite loud now, and it was difficult for Ereley to be heard over the sound. "We took a chance, capturing you, a very big chance. And it will be worth it, or you will be tossed aside as you have tossed so many of us aside."

"Are you going to overthrow the Pact?" She spoke more in disbelief than accusation. "Why should you? Daphne is part of the Pact."

"Is it? Is it really?" Ereley scoffed. "A strange way you have of showing our membership, Madame. You permit the Haiken Maru and other conglomerates to ship us off to planets where it doesn't suit you to work. You pay us wages that would be laughable if they were not tragic, and you say that because you permit a few of us to serve your purposes at higher ranks that you have included us in the Pact. We aren't even allowed to live on Earth without permits — given or sold by a human's whim!" He slammed down his hands on the back of the seat in front of him. The occupant swung around but never stopped chanting.

"But you are," said Jessine, belatedly beginning to fear the Daphnean. "You are all welcome in —" She stopped and went on more carefully. "My husband said that there were officials who took bribes to ignore the kinds of abuses you describe. But that isn't the way the Pact is supposed to work."

"Does that change anything, saying that we aren't *supposed* to be a source of cheap labor for humans?" Ereley gestured angrily. "You send us your advisors, with their guns and their soldiers, and you tell me that this is not the work of deliberate oppression?"

"That doesn't happen very often," said Jessine.

"What do you call often, Madame?" He indicated the other Daphneans in the aircar. "Ask them about relatives taken away at the whim of an advisor, about land seized and children pressed into service. Each one has endured something of the sort." He patted his armband. "This will make a change. The Rainbow will set us all to rights."

117

"And you are its leader?" she asked.

"I am the leader on this planet, but there are others, many others. We have already made progress in the Harmony Cluster. Governor Windsor supported equality. Governor Merikur supported Windsor — and now continues his campaign for equality. The Rainbow Dawn can — and will, if necessary — provide him with an army to enforce that equality." His eyes were bright, glazed with zeal.

"And my part?" asked Jessine.

"Your part will be to marry Governor Merikur. With your support, he can take the Secretariat. The Pact will continue, but will change, begin to grow again, as it has not for centuries."

"And if I choose not to support him?"

"Madame, I'd prefer not to discuss that possibility. After all, you are a sensible woman. Surely you understand that the Pact cannot survive much longer if it continues to abuse more than ninety percent of its population."

"Perhaps."

The driver of the aircar stopped chanting long enough to call out, "There is a fix being taken on us. Someone is tracking where we go."

"Who?" Ereley demanded, motioning to the others to chant more softly.

"I don't know. But the warning light came on

just now. Someone wants to know where we are." The driver pointed to the light on the front panel. "What do you want me to do?

"Keep a watch on it, and set our scanners to trace it back to its origin. I want to know if the tracker is moving or stationary." He cursed roundly in Daphnean, then abruptly became nonchalant. "It isn't that important, after all. If they know where we are, so much the better. It will help them realize how serious we are. We know how strong our position is. And it's stronger than any of you Senatorials think."

"How do you mean that?" asked Jessine, still unable to believe him.

"We have access to Kitchley's estate at Horizon Park, of course, and that means we can fight off attacks with a small force. I'll say this for Kitchley — he made a fortress of his estate. I doubt the Secretarial Palace was as well-armed as Kitchley's retreat. Well, it has to be now, doesn't it?" His amusement was emphatic and he stared at Jessine, challenging her to correct him or become angry.

"They will find you, Ereley. And when they do, no matter who is in power, they will take me back." Jessine masked the fear welling in her. She would not give them the pleasure of knowing how badly they frightened her. As she moved in her seat she felt her locket move under her shirt.

They were nearing the first boundaries of Horizon Park now, and two skirmisher aircars came up, demanding to know who was in the aircar and where it was bound. "If you are not authorized, turn back or we will be forced to shoot you down," said the nearer skirmisher.

"Under-Clerk Ereley, for Appointments Clerk Kitchley, to Kitchley's estate, the Orchid," he said, motioning the others to silence while the identification process was completed. "Escorting Madame Bouriere." He glared at her, daring her to contradict him.

"Voiceprint checks," said the skirmisher. "But we regret we do not have full release from Appointments Clerk Kitchley. The first signal was sent, but not the second."

Ereley stared out at the skirmishers. "What do you mean?" he asked.

The other Daphneans were instantly somber, and the driver looked anxiously from one skirmisher to the other.

"There must be a second release, which has not yet arrived." The skirmisher said. "We must request you land and wait until clearance is given."

"But," said Ereley, trying not to sound desperate, "We have Madame Bouriere with us. We are under orders to take her to the Orchid. We must have clearance at once."

The skirmishers swung back and forth across the aircar's bow. "You must remain where you are. We repeat. You must remain where you are. This is an official warning."

Ereley swore, then signaled to the others. "We have one chance. We have to take both of them down at once or we won't make it," he said.

The other Daphneans were upset and suddenly worried. Sankley spoke for all of them, saying, "We can't let this happen."

"Then shoot first and shoot straight," said Ereley, his features showing more pleasure than apprehension. He brought up his gun and aimed it though the window at the nearer skirmisher. "On the count of two. Everyone fire."

The Daphneans followed his orders quickly. Each one sighted on the power pods of the skirmishers.

"One," said Ereley. "Two."

The guns hammered and the skirmishers broke apart in twin explosions, raining flaming cinders on the barren stretch of land that bordered the woodlands of Horizon Park.

"You couldn't stop them recording your identification," said Jessine. "They know who you are and where you are going."

"It doesn't matter now," said Ereley as he signaled the driver to go on. "With any luck, the clerk who gets the message will be one of us and he'll lose the identification, at least for a while." He saw the startled expression she could not conceal. "You didn't think about that, did you? We're not the only ones in the Rainbow. There are thousands of us, thousands."

"What good will that do?" asked Jessine.

"We are ready. And when Anson Merikur orders it, we will rise. There is no service anywhere in the Pact where we have not found a niche. Governor Windsor will bring us equality, and we'll fight for him to achieve that." He had the look of a man who wanted the fight more than the equality.

"And the Cernians, the ones who tried to kidnap me, are they part of your Rainbow Dawn, too?" she asked.

Ereley made a sharp gesture. "No! No. They were, most likely, working for the Haiken Maru. The Cernian Confederation is as bad as the Pact. They've hired — or sold! — out to the Haiken Maru. They sell and enslave members of all species, including their own . . . When Governor Windsor is High Secretary, abuses of that sort will stop."

Jessine shrugged deliberately. "I don't think

that will be as simple as he thinks," she said in a tone filled with doubt and subtle contempt.

"Be quiet. You understand nothing." Ereley turned away from her and stared out the window as the aircar sped toward the Orchid.

Given a respite, Jessine looked down at the striations of specialized plantings in Horizon Park. Each region was specially planted and maintained, botanically and zoologically, with species from several planets set next to each other, protected by invisible barriers of electronic signals that kept each group of animals in its designated sector by generating a high, painful sound in the animals' skulls.

A fretwork of monorail tubes looked like a very simple spider web as the Daphnean aircar passed high overhead. Looking down, Jessine suspected that the monorail carried no sight-seers today.

"Take her lower," Ereley ordered the driver. "We don't want to be spotted by scanners."

"You will be," said Jessine.

"Perhaps," Ereley allowed. "But they're looking for overflights, not for something coming in for a landing. I know it's worked before."

Jessine did not reply, but sat quietly, watching the exotic scenery below and trying to think what she would do next.

There was a pride of Cernian blue lions drinking at a lake. Their huge heads appeared more enormous because of the standing ruff of thick, azure hair around their necks. Double tusks curled at the corners of their mouths; the Cernian lion had as much in common with a warthog as it did the big cats of Africa. Jessine watched them, momentarily distracted from her plight, admiring their grace.

Ereley noticed her gaze. "There are sand wolves down there, they tell me." He rubbed his long hands together. "In the Dellos section. Isn't the Orchid in the Dellos section?"

"I don't know," Jessine lied. "I've never been to the Orchid." The last part was true.

"Dellos sand wolves. They're known to be the most ferocious hunting animals in the Pact. I've seen them, on Dellos. No one wants to deal with them there. That's probably why they sent you so many for Horizon Park." He made the dry Daphnean equivalent of a chuckle. "A thank you for all your kindness to them."

Jessine looked at Ereley. "You're warning me about escaping. Shall we consider the warning given?"

"Oh, it bothers you to think about those creatures?" Ereley asked with false concern.

"It bothers me that you regard them with such

relish." She looked out over the Park, her attention fixed on the distant, hassock-like ferns from Peom. That environment contained some of the most beautiful plants and some of the most ferocious animals of any of the sectors of Horizon Park. Like the Peomers themselves, the animals were not large, but what they lacked in size they made up for in speed and rapacity. The Secretarial Retreat was in the Peom sector of the Park.

"Ah, I see the Orchid," said Ereley with genuine satisfaction. "And we are going to land in the outer court, between the double walls and the main compound itself."

The driver looked doubtful, but did his best to set his course as ordered.

"When we're out, drop the car into the other side of the estate. The others ought to be here," Ereley instructed the driver as they landed.

The ladders were lowered and the Daphneans made their way down them. Ereley and Jessine were last, and he ordered her to precede him.

It was windy as she started down the ladder, and not from the downdraft of the aircar alone. Now that she was out in the air, Jessine noticed that the trees some distance away were bending and tossing. That was not a good sign, for storms could cause serious disruptions at Horizon Park.

As they reached the ground, a large group of

Daphneans rushed up to greet Ereley, and to congratulate him on his prize.

"How many are here already?" asked Ereley, holding his gun on Jessine.

"About three hundred," said one who was clearly a second-in-command. "We're expecting more in the next hour." He motioned toward the massive doors of the fortress. "We had a little resistance when we arrived, but that's over with."

"Good." Ereley signaled to Jessine. "Come with us, Madame. We have prepared a room for you."

"How kind," said Jessine acidly, but she did as she was ordered. As she walked toward the door she saw four men — human soldiers — in Treasury uniforms lying side by side, a Peomer standing guard over them. There were fresh scars on the wall of the house and blackening at two of the windows where fires had been put out.

"It will be our headquarters until Governor Windsor arrives," said Ereley with pride. "We'll be unassailable."

"Do you think so?" said Jessine as she stepped onto the drawbridge. She noticed that there were two rainbow banners hanging in the inner courtyard.

The courtyard was crowded, most of the regular Orchid staff doing their best to be unnoticed.

They were predominantly Daphneans and Peomers, but there were Hillimots and a few humans as well. In addition there were the Daphneans of Rainbow Dawn, most of them relaxing in the first glow of victory. And in one corner, there were more than a dozen bodies laid out.

As they started to move, a section of the inner wall smashed to bits.

Ereley reacted immediately, swinging his gun into firing position, crouching as he jumped off the rim of the fountain. Another massive shell exploded on the second floor of the Orchid, spewing glastic and masonry onto the courtyard below.

"We're under attack," declared the second-in-command in complete disbelief.

"Get into positions!" ordered Ereley, already starting to move toward the massive gate to close it.

A third explosion smashed the fountain, and Ereley, struck by a flying stone flower, fell forward.

Now there were screams and shouts, and the second-in-command rushed to Ereley's side, bending over him. "He's alive!" he shouted as the next explosion rocked the courtyard.

Overhead three gunboats appeared out of the

southwest, the lowest of them bristling with laser-cannon and grenade launchers. They kept enough distance between themselves and the fortress to be at the limit of Kanovsky range.

There was panic in the courtyard now as all the staff tried to bolt for safety. The members of Rainbow Dawn attempted to stem the flight, though they were too disorganized to do much more than contribute to the rampant confusion around them.

Another shot ruined what was left of the fountain, and the water shot straight up into the air and fell onto the elaborate pattern of paving stones in the inner court.

Jessine had rushed to the shelter of the guard-post at the gate after the first shot.

The second-in-command started shouting orders. He was drowned out in a new explosion, this one collapsing the massive carved lintel over the out gate and destroying the mechanism to raise the drawbridge. Five bodies were blasted out of the gun station nearest the fountain, turning over in the air, delicate as birds until they landed.

Jessine hunched lower in the guard station and clapped her hands to her ears against the hideous noise. From the guard station, she could see a dreadnought coming toward the Orchid, its massive weapons trained on the estate. It fired a first shot at the outer wall, to establish range. The huge bricks collapsed into dust.

The Rainbow Dawn forces had their defenses up now, and a lucky shot took out the stabilizers in the nearest gunboat. It wobbled away, its complement of Navy fighting men dropping out of it in escape harnesses.

"Fire! Fire!" screamed Sankley, and was nearly bowled over as three panic-stricken Peomers rushed for the main gate.

A single blast from the dreadnought took out a large part of the south wall and shattered what remained of the windows.

Another blast from the dreadnought and another quadrant of the courtyard wall fell.

On the opposite side, the guard station no longer seemed much protection for Jessine. She ducked through it, into the outer court.

She looked around for a place to hide and, finding none, she turned east, away from the attacking Navy craft.

Jessine heard the next volley of firing and saw another section of the house heave, blast and fall to pieces. She kept going toward the outer walls, seeing only a few running Peomers and one exhausted Zambretic servant sitting on the grassy slope, gasping for breath and pounding the turf with all four of his fists. Another explosion behind her sent Jessine running for more protective distance between her and the main fortress.

A second dreadnought appeared, this one holding back, its cannon trained on the fortress, hovering in case more might was needed.

Jessine reached the breach in the walls and hesitated. She was safe from Rainbow Dawn now, but what of the Navy? What might Admiral Sclerida have in store for her if she remained within the grounds of the Orchid?

The dreadnought fired again, and this time the west side of the Orchid blew up. Without another qualm Jessine slipped through the gaping hole in the wall into the verdure of Horizon Park.

Chapter 9

Wiley was groggy from physical and emotional shock. He wiped his hand across his forehead, subconsciously trying to rub away present reality and return himself to the familiar round of wealth and privilege in which he'd spent his life until this terrible day.

The armored aircar didn't have windows, but

Wiley could see the forward vision screens past the shoulders of the driver and co-driver. The vehicle was slanting down toward a huge sky-colored dome in which the aircar's own reflection raced toward Wiley's eyes at redoubled speed.

They shot through the barrier into dimness rather than shattering impact. The dome was a polarizing bubble rather than a material wall. The shield not only protected the interior from observation, it combed sunlight and decreased the degree of illumination beneath the dome. Cernian eyes were adapted to much lower light levels than those of humans —

And almost all the figures Wiley saw within the domed enclosure were Cernians. There were hundreds of the aliens, driving equipment, unloading cargo and performing maintenance on the dozen or so starships on the ground within the domed starport. Perhaps there were more: the enclosed area was so large that moving figures were lost against its scale.

"This is Haiken Maru headquarters, isn't it?" demanded Wiley pugnaciously. "I know it is! The bubble north of the city is Haiken Maru headquarters!"

One of the Cernian guards blinked twice at him. The others didn't give even that much acknowledgement.

The aircar slowed. Besides barracks, sheds, and a maintenance hangar capable of holding one of the grounded starships, the headquarters complex included three hundred-story concrete warehouse towers. The aircar slowed further as the driver angled toward the landing pad on the roof of the central tower.

"We are arriving," one of the Cernians informed Wiley. It was the first time any of them had spoken since they had spirited Wiley away from the Kona Tatsu station.

"I can see that," said Wiley. He rubbed at his eyes, wondering if it was his hands or his face that felt so rough. The pilot set the aircar down and cut the engine. The silence was abrupt. Wiley had not been aware of how loud the aircar was until now.

"You will leave after I do," the Cernian informed him, holding a Meinhauser pistol aimed at the center of Wiley's chest.

"You bet," said Wiley. He tried not to shiver as he looked at the pistol, but he could not completely conceal his fear. His captors pushed him toward an access door. Air puffed out as the door opened: it was an airlock, and the pressure within was higher than ambient at this altitude.

Wiley stepped into the chamber in front of his guard. The outer door shut behind them and pressure built. The building was a sealed unit with enough positive internal air pressure to prevent gas or biotoxins from being introduced from the outside in the event of an attack.

"Move along," said the Cernian, gesturing with his Meinhauser as the inner door opened.

"I'm moving," said Wiley.

Beyond the airlock was a reception hall two stories high and domed with a tremendous stained glass window representing all the worlds on which the Haiken Maru traded. Beneath this, the room filled with priceless antiques, including a set of twenty-first century gaming tables, a full suit of armor, and in a place of honor, a genuine 1957 Cadillac in perfect condition, its doors open for those who wished to sit in it.

Wiley was still studying the eclectic but fascinating collection when the far door opened and a middle-aged man, broad of shoulder and broader of girth, stepped through. Wiley recognized Senator Lomax as the man extended his hand in welcome.

"Good afternoon, good afternoon, my lad," he cried merrily. "I'm very sorry about the inconvenience, but you understand we didn't have time to explain things when we rescued you."

Wiley stared at him. "Rescued?"

"Certainly, most certainly," said Senator

Lomax with all the sincerity he was capable of showing. "We couldn't have the Secretary's heir in the hands of the Kona Tatsu, now could we? No telling what those sly devils would do with you. Damien Ver doesn't have to account for how he handles his work. But that's going to change. Isn't it?"

"Is it?" Wiley asked, uncertain how to react to this affable reception.

"Well, of course it will," said Senator Lomax, at last grasping Wiley's hand and shaking it with fervor. "You're just the lad to make the change. And you'll find me ready to help you do it. You'll have all the support you could ask for. No more of this Kona Tatsu secrecy. Openness. That's the answer." He turned on his heel, indicating his remarkable collection. "Let me apologize for the atmosphere. This building has some special requirements, and I daresay you'll get used to it shortly. There's nothing harmful in the environmental adaptation, not for humans. People in trade get used to these things. Well, what do you think?"

This was much too fast for Wiley. He regarded Senator Lomax narrowly. He answered a question with a question of his own. "What's your plan? The Kona Tatsu's job is to protect me. What makes you think they'll give me up?"

Lomax kept smiling. "My dear boy, you must be starving. I'll have some dinner sent up right away."

Wiley had not missed *every* political dinner and knew an evasion when he heard one. He didn't think he'd be able to learn anything more from Lomax and he didn't pursue the question.

"Yes, thank you." But he kept his eyes open and tried to see everything.

Lomax left the room briefly, then returned with a bottle and a pair of glasses. "Dinner will be here shortly, but I thought you might like an apéritif." He set the glasses down on a marble-topped buffet and fumbled with the bottle's seals. "I couldn't trust this to the servants," he said. "Too precious."

Wiley wondered if the bottle might not have been safer in the hands of a servant. Lomax looked as though he might drop it at any moment.

"I must say," Lomax grunted, at last releasing the cork. "Your father's regrettable demise caught me a little unprepared. It was not expected, not so soon, at any case." He poured a golden liquid into the glasses and handed one to Wiley. "We — the Haiken Maru — had to speed up our operations to keep the Pact from failing. But we are prepared to support you, my lad, and we have the men to make you High Secretary within the next two days."

"Pardon me, but I believe that job belongs to the Kona Tatsu," replied Wiley. "They *are*, after all, the High Secretary's police."

Lomax frowned. "We have reason to believe that the head of the Kona Tatsu — Damien Ver, you know him — intends to try to take the Secretariat for himself."

Wiley rolled the stem of the glass between his fingers and studied the resulting small moments in the liquid. "I see. What do you intend to do about that?" He wasn't sure he believed Lomax, but didn't know Ver well enough to deny the charge.

"I have at my command right now over one hundred thousand Cernian mercenaries," replied Lomax. "Fully armed and with all necessary materiel. They are ready to stop this incursion from the Navy and place you at once at the head of the Secretariat. They will also defend you from the Kona Tatsu."

"Splendid," murmured Wiley. "I can see you have my best interests at heart."

"Certainly. Certainly. And for the moment, you really ought to relax. Let me provide a little entertainment for you." He made a signal and a concealed door opened.

There were five women, all different and all stunning. Each of them was dressed elegantly and each smiled at him as if there were no one else in the room.

"Let me say that the Cernians are utterly loyal to Haiken Maru," said Senator Lomax, convinced that Wiley could not possibly be concentrating on his words. "We hold their contract, and without our endorsement there is nowhere on Earth they can go or hide."

The fairest of the women reached Wiley and slid her arms around him, placing her soft lips at the corner of his mouth. She was shapely and pliant, fitting her body against his as if there were no clothes between them.

Senator Lomax sipped at his drink. "There is a small chamber to which you might wish to retire."

The woman holding Wiley nodded and tugged him toward an elaborate gold-chased door. He followed, setting his glass, untouched, on the hood of the '57 Cadillac.

The AID Nika had given him at the safe house broke away from one of its belt loops. Wiley grabbed for it. The other loop broke and the whole unit fell to the floor.

The AID's casing crumbled. It was as rotten as ice that's been sitting for weeks in sub-freezing temperatures, subliming directly from solid into gas without passing through a liquid state.

A human in coveralls with orange and yellow Haiken Maru collar flashes burst into the reception hall from a side door. One of the women caressing Wiley began to scream. Behind the shouting human was a Cernian whose garments were slick with blood.

The alien collapsed in the doorway, jamming the panel open. In the corridor beyond him were three more Cernians, fallen and hemorrhaging through their skin. Purple-tinged blood pooled on the tiles beneath them. Their eyes and tongues protruded. One of the aliens thrashed mindlessly; the other two bent backward in bone-breaking convulsions.

Only dusty traces remained of the AID's casing. The plastic had begun to decay into gases toxic to Cernian metabolisms as soon as Wiley brought the unit into the higher atmospheric pressure of the sealed building. Nika — the Kona Tatsu — had used him as a Trojan horse!

Senator Lomax waved a control stylus. Vision screens flashed from behind panels all around the reception hall. Each screen displayed a different facet of the reality universal within the immense building: Cernians dying in blood and agony.

Lomax pointed his stylus at Wiley. "You did this!" the Senator shouted. "*You* did this! Kill him!"

The aide who'd been too horror-struck to report intelligently now scrabbled at the pistol holster hanging from his belt. One of the women tried to grab Wiley. Wiley knocked her aside and bolted for the doorway.

Another human was coming toward him from the other end of the corridor. "Where are you going?" the Haiken Maru employee demanded. "Who are —"

Bullets from the reception hall ripped the cornice molding above Wiley's head. The second human drew his pistol with an inarticulate shout. Wiley leaped into the dropshaft in the middle of the corridor, then dodged out at the next level down.

And into a precinct of Hell.

Weapons and materiel of all sorts lay strewn amid the bodies of violently convulsing Cernians. Huge lesions were opening in many of the bodies, and grotesquely swollen organs protruded as the aliens contorted in unspeakable agony.

He couldn't bring himself to pick up any of the guns lying there for the taking, not if it meant getting any closer to the dying Cernians. He ran as quickly as he could, taking care where he stepped. Twice he slid on welling blood and once a feeble Cernian hand almost closed on his ankle.

Finally through the gloom Wiley spotted another dropshaft, turned and dashed for it, as much to escape the carnage around him as to put more distance between him and any pursuers. As he reached the dropshaft he consulted the levels: 104 to G. He rode it all the way to Level 1.

There were Cernians here as well. Thick mucus ran from their eyes and their dying bodies were slick with blood. The stench was hideous. On the far side of the expanse of dying and dead aliens there were humans, armed and determined, and shooting at him.

To his right, almost against one wall, there were sleek Cobra tanks. At the head of the phalanx, one of them was purring, idling in this charnel vault.

Wiley raced for it with all the speed he possessed, hoping that if any of the bullets struck, they would kill him at once; he did not want to die slowly in all this wretchedness.

There was a Cernian driver in the tank, his chest burst open, his arms slick with blood. He was not quite dead. Wiley hesitated, but the shooting didn't, so he dragged the alien out of the tank. Hurriedly, he climbed in, and without bothering to try to figure out how to close the hatch, slipped into the driver's position. He set the huge machine in motion, heading toward the loading bay's tremendous doors. He could hear bullets and grenades bouncing off the armored hide of the tank, and he began to hope that he would make it out after all.

The door buckled, moaned, and gave way as Wiley smashed the Cobra directly at its center.

Only then did he realize that the G on the dropshaft indicated Ground, not Garage, and he was hurtling out into a twenty foot drop with an expanse of port paving below.

Chapter 10

Chaney had pulled himself up onto the skid and was clinging with all his limbs. He wasn't sure how much longer he could hold on. He reached up and pounded on the underside of the hull, hoping Tira could hear and would do something.

In fact, the aircar's motion was so erratic that

Tira thought it was damaged. She was wondering if she dared set down. No, she was all alone; Sclerida would catch her. She heard pounding and checked her bottom view mirror. It was Chaney. She opened the hatch; maybe Chaney would be able to climb in. She dared not cut her speed to aid him.

Chaney heard the hatch open above him. It was a few moments before he had the courage to look. Maybe . . .

He stretched. Reached for a handhold inside the door. One hand in. Good.

Tira heard him behind her and finally put the controls on auto. She reached him as he was trying to throw a leg into the cabin. She grabbed the leg and pulled.

"Ouch!" The rest of him bumped and tumbled over the threshold and into the aircar. Tira fell back against the opposite bulkhead.

"You okay?" she asked, catching her breath.

"Fine," answered Chaney. "My favorite way to board an aircar."

"Try not to be so late next time," she replied.

Stumbling to his feet, Chaney closed the hatch. Tira rose also and they embraced silently.

"Are you really okay?" she finally asked.

"Really," he answered. "A little bruised, no problem. How about you?"

"I'm okay." She sat back in the pilot's chair and took the controls back to manual. "A little confused."

Chaney dropped into the copilot's seat and sighed. "Yeah. It's like this. My parents split. I stayed with my mother and my brother Dov went with *him* . . . with our father. I kept my mother's name. I guess I took her side, too, but . . . well, she was right and he was a slime mold. Still is. An ambitious slime mold."

"I thought you meant he was dead."

"I know. I'm sorry. It's just . . . I wanted to love him. He was my father, you know? And then . . . I guess he didn't really change. I just found out things I hadn't known about him. It was like losing him. I didn't want him to be my father anymore."

Tira considered. "I guess," she said after a while, "that in that respect I haven't really lost my father. He's still my father. It's just his physical presence I've lost." Her voice caught at the end of her sentence and Chaney reached out a hand.

"I'm sorry," he said.

She shook her head. "I've got to pull myself together. Figure out what to do next."

Chaney nodded, squeezed her hand and let go. "Do you have a destination in mind? We should really ditch this car; they've almost certainly got a tracer on it."

Tira grimaced. "Not good. But actually, I do have a plan," she said, and there was a little mischief back in her smile. "If they're tracing us, and if you think they might have plans, then we might as well go right back to the Secretarial Palace." Her smile did not hold up through her last few words, but her resolution was clear.

"What?" said Chaney, unable to sit upright harnessed into his couch.

"Because," she went on with purpose, "I've been thinking about it, and I suspect that is the place they would least expect me to go. Besides, the Palace is so confused they won't be able to mount much of a search for us. They'll have their hands full just getting in the front door."

"And what about us?" asked Chaney, although he was beginning to see the sense of her plan.

"I know the Palace very well, and I know where we can hide out if we have to." She did not add that she hoped that one or two of her staff had survived and might be hiding in the Palace, as well.

"What do you mean?" Chaney was wary now.

"There are secret passages in the walls. They're for the Kona Tatsu. My father showed me where they are and how to reach them."

He could not help but agree with her. "All right. It makes sense."

"I thought we'd set down outside the walls. There's bound to be people from the city who've come out to watch the fighting, and to do what they can to use it to advantage. We could —"

"You mean you expect looters? So soon?" Chaney was amazed at how calmly she suggested it.

"I'd be a fool not to," she said. "And it could mean we'd have a better chance to arrive unnoticed. If we try to set down inside the walls, even in a Navy aircar, someone might pay attention."

"But outside, there would be other aircars, and —"

"And every kind of vehicle you can imagine. If we arrive in this, no one will think anything of it. It will be just one more aircar. And if we leave it where there are many others, then when the Navy follows the tracer, they'll have to sort through the confusion." She glanced at him. "Not too bad, do you think?"

"It could work," Chaney allowed.

"And it wouldn't be risky. Under the circumstances, Lieutenant, I think it's the best we can come up with."

"All right, then. I'll check our supplies here." He rose and went back to find the weapons lockers.

"Plenty of weapons," he called to her, pulling

out two railguns with shoulder straps. On further reflection, he pulled out two more. Two people, two shoulders each. He opened another locker: half a dozen bandoliers of railgun ammunition. Very nice.

The next locker held ration kits and Chaney suddenly realized how hungry he was. He brought his finds forward.

"Hungry?" He held a ration bar in front of Tira's mouth.

"Ick," she said, shying away. "What's that?"

"Food," he answered. Somehow, he'd almost forgotten that she wasn't a soldier. "Rations. Portable feast."

"Good Lord," she said. "That's what we feed our soldiers?"

"Yup." He sat down and took a bite of his own ration bar.

"No wonder the Navy's mutinied." She wrinkled her nose and Chaney's heart gave a little jump.

Tira finally bit into the ration bar. "Guess it's better than starving," she conceded.

Chaney laughed, an amazing feeling of pure delight coming over him.

"We'll be fine," he said. "Somehow, one way or another, we'll be fine."

They rode on toward the Palace.

❖   ❖   ❖

They landed the aircar on the far side of the Senatorial building from the Palace. There were dozens of aircars parked there and they hoped the crowd would slow down any pursuers.

They made their way around the Senatorial building and across the open plaza to the Palace. There were crowds in the plaza: civilians of all classes, fighting, screaming, walking in stunned silence; and soldiers: Secretarial Guard, Navy — Logistics and Protectorate both — and a few plain black Kona Tatsu uniforms. Chaney and Tira shoved through the crowds, clutching their weapons and watching for trouble.

Finally they entered the Palace itself. Here the bustle was greater, not less. Clerks moved through the halls at a frantic pace, carrying papers, boxes, and even furniture. Tira couldn't tell if they were looting or doing their jobs.

They reached a dropshaft without incident, which Tira admitted made her suspicious. "There's only one place to go with this, the cross-over. No other stops."

"Let's try it," said Chaney.

Tira stepped into the dropshaft and activated it, relieved when it actually worked.

They reached the cross-over in seconds, and found the whole of the long connecting tunnel a mass of scattered debris and abandoned dead. Most of the bodies were aliens — Daphneans and Peomers — but there were clerks and Treasury uniforms among them.

"It must have been quite a fight," said Chaney.

"Look at that on the wall. Rainbow Dawn. What does that mean?"

Tira pointed to the huge scrawled letters.

"Don't ask me," said Chaney, and started cautiously down the cross-over toward the south-east tower.

They had reached the tower when three clerks rushed out on them, holding chairlegs for clubs and blocking their way.

"You can't come in. No one can come in." The clerk nearest them took a frightened, brave step forward. "Leave. Now."

"We're both armed. We have guns," said Chaney patiently, not wanting to hurt the terrified clerks.

Tira did not step back either. "But I live here," she said simply.

The clerk stared at her. "Thousands of people live here," he blustered. "That means nothing."

"It does to me," said Tira. "And it must to you, or you would have left with the others."

The nearest clerk looked perplexed. "Well, someone has to keep order. We can't all run away or it would all be . . . lost."

"Yes," said Tira, taking a step nearer the clerk. "I've been trying to get back here since the first attack yesterday. Do you think you could let me and my guard through, if we give you our words that we won't do any damage?"

As she came closer, the clerk suddenly recognized her. He turned to the others. "What do you think?"

They were too scared to speak, but one of them nodded.

"All right. Go through." The clerk kept his chairleg at the ready. "If anything happens, it will be on your head."

"Fine," said Chaney, and followed Tira down the hall.

"That was taking quite a chance," he said to her as they moved out of earshot.

"Those clerks are the ones taking the chance. We could have killed them." She was very serious. "They have a lot of courage, staying here, defending the Palace. They could be looting, but they're not. They're the kind of people my father wanted the Pact for."

They found a relatively isolated lift tube and stepped in, Tira in the lead.

"Do you know where we are?" asked Chaney.

"Yes. In fact, if I recall properly, we're headed someplace safe. I hope."

The lift tube led to the nursery.

"I haven't been up here for years. I'll bet Wiley hasn't either," said Tira. "Jessine hasn't given my father any heirs, thank heavens; it's probably been forgotten."

The genescan monitor was still working. It politely informed them that it required authorization before the doors could be opened. Tira put her hand on the scanner and winced when the machine said, "Missy Tira-Lira. How good to see you again."

"Missy Tira-Lira?" Chaney asked as they went through the door.

"I was a kid," she answered defensively.

All the furniture was moved against the walls and shrouded in dustsheets. No toys lay on the floor, none of the teaching displays were on. After the ravishment of the rest of the Palace, these neglected apartments seemed pleasantly serene.

"Forgotten?" remarked Chaney, pointing down.

There were footprints in the dust.

He swung up one of his railguns. "Wait," he said quietly, and followed the footprints. Tira shouldered one of her own guns and backed him up.

The footprints led through a doorway and

behind a giant stuffed gorilla. Chaney stopped several feet from the toy.

"Come out with your hands up," he said.

There was a single shriek, and then a gowned figure appeared from behind the gorilla, hands raised, calling tearfully, "Please, don't shoot."

Tira gave a joyful yelp and let her weapon hang from its strap. "Cousin Helga!" She passed Chaney to go to her cousin.

"Tira!" exclaimed the old lady, and opened her arms to embrace Tira. "Oh, my dear," she said, weeping unashamedly. "Oh. Oh, gracious. It really is you."

Chaney stared, baffled.

"She's my cousin, Chaney," explained Tira. "I thought you were dead, Helga. What are you doing here?"

The old woman looked flustered, then sighed heavily. "I know I should have stayed in your quarters. But I couldn't . . . bear to clean it up. Half the outer wall was gone, and there were bodies everywhere. There was blood on the ceiling. I . . . I couldn't bear it, Tira. So I came up here. Just until things settled down."

"That was very sensible of you," said Tira.

Cousin Helga shook her head. "No. No, I'm afraid I've been very foolish. If I hadn't given the Treasury men access to your chambers, none of this would ever have happened."

"*You* gave the Treasury access —?" Tira demanded, too amazed to be outraged.

"They said you were in danger, you see. They said the Haiken Maru was going to kidnap you. Or worse. Kitchley informed me of the trouble, and we agreed that the Treasury officers were the ones to protect you. But . . . but it turned out so very badly." She started to cry again.

Tira put her arm around Cousin Helga's shoulder. "Don't cry, dear. You mustn't cry. Please don't cry."

Chaney came closer to them, looking down at Cousin Helga. "I'm afraid Kitchley was wrong," he said as kindly as he could. "It wasn't the Haiken Maru who did this." His eyes turned somber. "It was Admiral Sclerida who killed the High Secretary."

Cousin Helga stared at Chaney in shock. "Admiral Sclerida?"

Chaney's voice hardened. "The High Secretary was killed on his order. I'm certain of it."

"Chaney," said Tira, but she wasn't as shocked as she thought she should be.

Cousin Helga began to cry in earnest.

Chapter 11

Thick underbrush offered Jessine cover almost as soon as she'd slammed the fire door behind her. She moved away through the brush, taking care to leave as little trail as possible. In spite of the battle, she feared she might still be pursued, for if Governor Merikur should arrive with troops, the tables might easily be turned on the attackers.

She found a creek and decided to follow it. Very soon, she came to a boundary fence. It was essentially invisible, consisting of squat pillars of metal and stone spaced about every hundred meters. The pillars contained transmitters that sent signals to the pain centers of Horizon Park's animal inhabitants. The transmitters allowed for a buffer of about a hundred meters between strips, a sort of no-beast's-land where pain implants ruled.

Jessine followed the stream through the buffer and into the next strip. She was now in the Hillimot sector, a thickly wooded place with a variety of evergreen-type trees and flowers the size of platters. There were flying creatures here, as brightly colored as tropical parrots but more closely resembling large bats. After the chaos of the Palace and then Kitchley's house, the sector seemed peaceful, and Jessine let herself be entranced by its beauty and calm.

A wail, sharp and high, broke that calm.

Jessine went very still. There were bauins in this sector, she remembered — long, leggy predators of stealthy habits and relentless appetites. They hunted in packs, surrounding their prey and making escape impossible.

She stepped into the stream. The water would help keep the bauins from smelling her. She hoped the bauins hunted by smell.

The sound of the bauin was echoed by another. Stream or no stream, they seemed to be coming closer. She clutched at her rifle, then picked up a rock instead. Maybe she could divert it.

She threw the rock. It crashed into the underbrush and the wails stopped for a moment. She picked up another rock.

She stood still for several moments, but could not hear any more bauin calls. She slogged forward in the creek. Somewhere up ahead there had to be a monorail station, and when she found it, she would be safe. Might be safe, anyhow.

A hundred yards farther on, the creek became a small river. In places the bank was too steep for her to walk and she had to swim, and hope her weapons survived. After the first dunk, she ditched the poncho. It wasn't heavy, but it dragged at her and hindered her strokes.

A pillar on either side, and the river rolled into the next sector: Dellos.

At once the environment changed, the vegetation more sparse and pulpier. There were few trees, and those stood near the river. Standing along the banks was a small herd of loose-limbed sylees, high-shouldered and narrow-haunched. They were formidable leapers, a necessary survival trait for the favorite prey of sand wolves, the rail-thin coursing carnivores called ninikik on Dellos.

Jessine swam slowly, rolling over now and then to check for signs of sand wolves.

The sylees kept their heads moving between drinks, and ambled restlessly from one spot to another, always prepared to run.

The river was growing louder. Jessine knew there was a canyon ahead, and rapids. She wanted to leave the water now, before it got any faster and the walls of the canyon trapped her.

Jessine could see the first drop-off of rapids a short distance ahead in the river, and she fought her way toward the shore. But the river was strong and fast now, and she smashed into a shoal of hidden rocks, bruising her legs. Her arms scraped on a boulder as she strove to grab hold of it, but she refused to let the pain loosen her grip, and this time she did not get pulled from safety.

Slowly, aching from the battering in the river, she dragged herself onto the rock, and sat there a short while to inspect her bruises. Sighing at the colors she knew would come later, she rose and started up the slope for the plateau over the canyon.

It was a long canyon, growing deeper for fifteen miles, and then slowly giving way to the rocky slopes at the back of Horizon Park, more than thirty miles away. Jessine had often seen it from the air but had never been this close to it. The canyon divided the Dellos Sector from the Daphnean sector. At its far end there was a fairly good-sized settlement where the families of the Horizon Park maintenance staff lived, but that was too far and they might well be Rainbow Dawn adherents.

The monorail was still her best bet, but she still had not caught sight of it, and she fumed at the planners of the Park, who had been at such pains to be sure the monorail was not intrusive.

Coming to high ground, she paused. As she turned in a circle, a bright flicker caught the corner of her eye. She focused on it. Back toward Kitchley's house, something was burning. She wondered how fast the fire would spread.

Behind her, suddenly, she heard the eerie chuckle of sand wolves who've found their prey.

She whirled, lifting her rifle to firing position, but the wolves had found something else to eat. Jessine bolted, heading for the sector line. If she could reach the buffer before the wolves killed their meal, she might be able to rest safely.

Safely. If you could call it safe to be caught between sets of wild beasts. *No more dangerous, in a way,* she thought, *than being caught between two — or more — sets of wild political factions*. At least the beasts would simply eat her and be done with it.

She spotted the transmitter pillars and pushed herself harder. Meters before of the boundary, she stopped short. A Cernian spabot, massive, mauve and scaly, stood beside a pillar, honking in surprise.

Jessine stared at the beast, and realized that the power had failed, for the spabot was on Dellos sector ground.

The power station! thought Jessine. *Someone must have hit it!*

She moved as quickly as she could to get out of the path of the tremendous animal, watching its nervous progress as she went.

The chuckles of the sand wolves stopped.

The spabot made its ponderous way forward, armored head lowered defensively, long, rough-scaled tail flicking.

Then the sand wolves appeared over a ridge and ran directly at the spabot. Two of them leapt to sink teeth into the meaty shoulder.

The huge tail slapped the first wolf away, and the second could not sink his teeth into the thick, loose hide.

As the spabot lashed his tail again, the end slapped Jessine across the shoulders, sending her staggering, black spots forming before her eyes.

The sand wolves began to circle the spabot, one or two of them eyeing Jessine speculatively. She raised her rifle and put her bruised back against the pillar.

A new cry brought her head around. A hunting pack of Cernian blue lions had come from the trees to find their planned spabot dinner under attack. They were displeased.

The spabot made a short lunge at the sand wolves, and this time one of the Dellos wolves took hold, sinking his curved fangs deep into the huge upper lip of the spabot.

With a rumbling squeal the spabot swung its tail in frenzy and attempted to pull the sand wolf off.

Jessine swung the rifle from threat to threat.

Overhead there was the sound of an aircar. It dropped down to hover above the fighting beasts. The hatch opened and someone opened fire. A path opened between Jessine and the aircar, but she wasn't sure she wanted to trade her wild beasts for wild politicians.

"Jessine! Stop daydreaming and get in here!"

It was Damien Ver. Her mind hesitated, but her heart didn't. She rushed to the ladder he held for her, and dragged herself up it and into his arms.

Chapter 12

The tank slammed into the pavement. Its nose was buried in the ground, and the tank teetered for a moment. Inside, Wiley took the shock against an expanding gel cocoon. Before he had quite registered what had happened, the pavement lost its grip and the tank slammed down to horizontal. The treads squeaked as they caught at the surface and then the power died.

Catching his breath, Wiley pushed out of the gel cocoon and through the still-open hatch.

He ducked back in as gunfire snapped around him. More cautiously, he peeked over the edge. There were human guards in gas masks standing in the doorway of the warehouse. Senator Lomax was there, waving his arms and shouting. Wiley dropped back into the tank and tried to think.

The shouting continued. He put his head in his hands. Why was all this happening? Because he had been born the son of the High Secretary. It suddenly occurred to him that it wouldn't matter if it were someone else, if *he* were a different person — as long as he wore the body of the son of the High Secretary, he would be a target. Nothing personal.

And suddenly, all the lack of personal involvement struck him. There *was* nothing personal, about this attack, or about his life. He hung with Dov Sclerida and that crowd, or they with him, really, because he was the High Secretary's son, not because he was a person. No girl had ever taken an interest in him, only in the heir to the Secretariat. Nothing he had ever done, or which had been done for him, no conversation, nothing of his life had any meaning or value outside of his existence as the High Secretary's heir.

"Splendid," he said to himself. "I don't even want the damned chair."

But he did want some kind of life, so he'd better get moving before someone came to get him. Once again he raised his head slowly out of the tank.

And once again gunfire ripped through the air around him. This time, though, there was answering fire. He turned to see an open patrol car, carrying a pair of Cernians, rake light cannon fire across the warehouse doorway. The humans fell, Lomax included, and the aircar slid inside the warehouse. Wiley watched as the two guards jumped out of the aircar and started to cross to his tank. Clearly, they intended to rescue what they thought was a Cernian comrade. He heard their shouts of anger as they surveyed the carnage — dead Cernians everywhere.

"Betrayal!" he heard them howl, before the last remnants of the gas caught them and rendered them mute.

Wiley looked around. His tank was dead. The only options he had were to walk — not an appealing choice — or to go back into the warehouse and take the patrol car. Shuddering, he climbed out of the tank and ran for the service ladder.

When he re-entered the loading bay, the sight made his stomach turn. All this, because the High Secretary had an heir. And because he was that heir, he had to endure, to see it, to know it was for him. Swallowing hard, he turned away and took the patrol car.

Speeding around the complex, he looked for the seam, barely visible, where the two screens of the e-mag shield met. Passing it, he zipped around another quarter of the shield. There, halfway between the seams, should be a generator. He hoped it wasn't buried too deeply. He opened fire with half of the patrol car's arsenal. After a few seconds, there was the sound of shattering syncrete and sparks jumped from his target area. Then the shield flickered and went down. Wiley turned and sped away.

Chapter 13

Ver gave Jessine one quick fierce kiss before pushing her toward the copilot's seat. Taking the pilot's seat himself, he pulled the aircar out of its hover.

"How are you?" he demanded. "Injuries?"

Jessine shook her head, dazed by the sudden sense of safety. "Bruises. Nothing broken, I

think. How did you find me? How goes the —
war?" she asked.

Ver took one hand from the controls to lift
Jessine's cameo on a fingertip. "There's a tracer
in this," he said, his eyes on his flying.

"But what if I hadn't worn it today!" Jessine
gasped.

The Kona Tatsu chief shrugged. "If you hadn't
worn the gift I'd asked you always to wear . . ." he
said without emotion. "That would have been
your decision, wouldn't it?"

Jessine realized then, as she had never fully
appreciated before, that while Damien Ver
wasn't as cold as others thought him, her lover
was as implacable as lava welling from the heart
of a volcano. His will was a force of nature.

"As for the 'war,'" he continued mildly, "it
won't get that far. In fact, the situation is under
control and very close to over." He pushed the
aircar higher. Jessine thought its response was
sluggish.

She raised an eyebrow. "The Navy is attacking
an alien rights group in a high official's residence,
the Palace is under attack by Cernians, the High
Secretary is dead and the situation is under *control*?"

"It's not the Navy, it's only Logistics branch
under Sclerida and Logistics is being overcome.

The Cernians in the Palace are dead, and . . . well, we still don't know precisely where the heir is. But, yes, the situation is under control.

"We *do* know that the Haiken Maru are out of the game. There was an explosion and the shield went down at their main complex and we were able to clean up there."

The tracking screen bleeped. Jessine looked over to see four dots appear, indicating ships in pursuit. An instant later, the screen had identified the pursuers as Haiken Maru.

"Damien," she said, gesturing at the screen. "Has anyone *told* the Haiken Maru that they're out of the game?"

Ver glanced at the screen. "Fools. They've got to know they've lost. Their primary puppet is dead and ninety-six percent of their top staff are under arrest.

"Ninety-six percent?" Jessine wasn't sure if she was shocked or not.

Ver nodded. "We'll get the others. It's just a matter of time."

Jessine nodded, watching the blips on the screen. They were definitely in pursuit, and gaining. "Who killed Lomax?"

"Unclear as yet. There were a lot of messily dead Cernians on the scene. Maybe their contract expired. In any case, that's one faction down. Sclerida's men have lost a number of battles to loyal Naval forces. He's not going to win."

The blips for the four aircars behind them kept growing closer on the rear screen. She indicated their pursuers. "I thought you said that things are under control."

"I did," he said. "And they are."

"Un-huh," said Jessine with a significant glance toward the rear.

"I meant it," Ver said with determination. "But the matter isn't ended yet, and there might be a few more difficulties before this is over."

"A few more difficulties like being shot out of the sky," she said bluntly.

"That would be one," he agreed. "And I don't want that to happen." He saw the communications scanner come alight and he studied the jumble displayed there, his AID automatically translating the code. "Until a few hours ago, very few people knew what was actually going on. There's been an emergency block on news, and the military reports are often misleading. Our biggest trouble is confusion. I've been relying on the Kona Tatsu agents in the military services to help rectify this."

"And support the Kona Tatsu position," said Jessine.

"Naturally; that's their job," said Ver without

apology. He shoved a lever to increase the strength of their shields.

Two seconds later a pair of missiles swept by, deflected just in time. Two seconds after that the warheads burst in Horizon Park, setting a stretch of conifer forest ablaze. Ver banked the aircar toward one of the small support villages at the edge of Horizon Park. "I'm scanning these places for Rainbow Dawn transmitters. They're going to need to be isolated."

Jessine could not keep from shuddering. "Rainbow Dawn," she repeated.

"Kitchley got away with it for several years, but once they became really active, he should have known we'd find him out." He dropped a little lower over the village, watching the display on the right side of the control panel. "Using his own estate was a foolish thing to do. He should have realized that would give him away."

"Kitchley?" Jessine said indignantly. "He was never their leader. Kitchley was killed by Rainbow Dawn. I saw them do it. The one in charge is Ereley. He told me about what they were trying to do." She felt a twinge of grief for her Daphnean friend who had been so loyal to her, and had been murdered for his loyalty.

"What are you saying?" Ver demanded as he

checked the screens in front of him. "It wasn't Kitchley? You mean he was set up?"

"Yes," said Jessine. "Absolutely. He was the Rainbow Dawn sacrificial goat. If they get any power in a few months they'll probably convey an official martyrdom on Kitchley. Ereley is . . . or was the head. He's made arrangements with Governor Windsor and Anson Merikur to change the government, with Rainbow Dawn providing the support."

"Instead of the Kona Tatsu?" Ver asked with a wicked chuckle.

"Instead of Haiken Maru, I suspect," she corrected him, stretching as much as the harness would allow to try to ease the hurt in her muscles. She was going to need a long massage and half a dozen therapy baths before she would be free of the ache.

Ver nodded. "Or a combination of the two. For all their claims of equality, it's apparent that Rainbow Dawn has several classes of equality in their reform schemes." He swung the aircar to port, feeling it wallow as it responded.

"Is this vehicle going to make it?" Jessine asked.

"I think so," he answered cautiously. "It will get us back to the Secretarial Palace."

She blanched. "Why would we want to go back there?"

"Because that's where we have the command bunkers and where the most communication equipment is. Right now communication is the most important weapon we possess. That's why we're winning and the others are losing."

"Including Admiral Sclerida?" Jessine inquired with false sweetness.

"Jessine, I've said so. If we can keep his forces in confusion, he will continue to lose." He leveled off again, and checked the proximity of their pursuers. "That's the focus of what the Kona Tatsu is doing with the Navy right now."

"But he might still pull it off," said Jessine.

"He might," Ver allowed. "If he is able to capture *and keep* either you or Tira. If either of you were forced to marry him, or Tira was forced to marry Dov, his claim to the succession would be upheld." He frowned at the latest coded display. "Scratch that last option," he said as his implant translated the latest information.

"What is it?" Jessine asked.

"We've just found the wreckage of a Logistics vessel in the city. It's full of dead Navy personnel and Dov Sclerida." He watched the display. "We have genescan confirmation. Dov Sclerida is dead." He shook his head. "Poor kid. He didn't deserve —"

"He didn't deserve any of his life. Admiral

172

Sclerida only wanted kids so he'd have pawns for the game," Jessine said cynically. "I remember one got away from him."

"The Chaney lad. His mother saw to that, sensible woman that she was," said Ver with evident approval. "I've never met him, but his files are very satisfactory."

He tried another maneuver, straining the ship's power to the maximum.

"It isn't over yet, though?" remarked Jessine. The four dots were closing more rapidly.

"Not yet," he said. "But it's closer to being over than most people know. The Haiken Maru is out of the game permanently. Logistics has two moves until checkmate."

"But those two moves could change things. If Sclerida captures either Tira or me." She shivered suddenly.

"Captures and *keeps*. From what I've seen yesterday and today, that's not easy to do." His smile was warm, suffused with pride for her. "You're not the ornament Sclerida thinks you are."

"He thinks all women are ornaments," said Jessine contemptuously.

"And half the boys in the world as well," added Ver. He stared at the next coded information. "No sign of Tira yet. None of the Kona Tatsu in

Logistics cover have heard anything about her. There was a rumor she was at Sclerida's residence, but that's —"

"Absurd," said Jessine. "How would she get there and if she did get there, how could Sclerida not announce it?"

"Exactly. And there's an unsubstantiated report that Admiral Sclerida has left there himself, which I doubt he would do if he had Tira." He looked at the side screens and cursed.

"We're being boxed in," said Jessine.

"It's insane, doing this," said Ver, adding under his breath, "There's no point in Haiken Maru trying something this foolish now."

Over their hailer came clipped instructions to hover and leave the aircar, with the assurances they would not be harmed if they obeyed promptly.

"They're going to regret this," said Ver as he slowed his aircar while he looked for a clear space to set down.

"Oh, don't," said Jessine, at last disheartened and weary. "Let's get it over with."

"This really is for the best, darling," said Ver.

He informed the four Haiken Maru cars of the site he had selected. "There's enough room for you to land, two on either side," he added through gritted teeth.

"Acceptable," came the response.

"You'd better land. We'll have to hover; there's some trouble with the drive-fans or stabilizers. Something isn't right with the gyroscopes." He paused.

"We saw you were having trouble," said one of the leaders. "Tough luck."

The four Haiken Maru aircars touched down, two on either side of Ver's aircar.

"Fortunes of war," said Ver, and turned to Jessine. "I'm going to lower the equipment ramp. Make sure you raise your hands when you go down it."

"Can't we self-destruct?" she asked, trying to laugh but unable to hide her serious intent.

"Stand here, and I'll set the scanner to show them we're surrendering." He activated the hailer. "We'll be coming out with hands raised. There is an electronic record now of our surrender, here and at Kona Tatsu command." He winked at her, and added softly. "Now they can't claim any resistance or accidental injury."

"If you say so," she told him listlessly.

"Don't worry, Jessine," he said seriously. "It's going to be all right."

"Oh, yes. I'll be forced to marry Admiral Sclerida or Governor Merikur and you'll be banished or killed. It couldn't be better." She raised her hand once, then lowered it. "We might as well get this over with."

"Yes," he said.

They started toward the loading ramp, Jessine behind Ver. To her the open hatch loomed like the grave.

Then it seemed Ver tripped; at least he stumbled a little and reached out to one of the seats to steady himself.

There was a sudden rush. Ver turned at once and flung himself on Jessine throwing her backward and covering her with his body.

The air around them rocked and thrummed and all four of the Haiken Maru aircars flew to bits in a welter of spectacular flames. The disintegrated bits spattered against Ver's aircar's hull; the rest was vaporized and vanished in a broad wash of chemical brilliance.

Ver propped himself on his elbows and beamed at her as he smoothed the splendid tangle of hair back from her face. "Short-range missiles," he said. "I installed two of them where the auxiliary drive fans usually are. Just in case."

Chapter 14

In the living room of Tira's suite the floor was still unswept and the furniture in ruins, but between Cousin Helga and Tira, Tira's bedroom was now reasonably neat. The bed was made and Cousin Helga was setting about the tedious task of finding out how much of Tira's wardrobe was still useable.

Chaney had elected to stay in the rubble of the living room and repair the communications panel. If he were lucky, his AID would be able to ferret out some information on the overall situation. "But I haven't been able to break into Naval Logistics records," he admitted to Tira.

"Maybe they've dumped all the information," said Tira. She and Helga were starting in on the mess that was the living room. "If they have, then —"

"Oh, they haven't," said Chaney with certainty. "They've squirreled it away somewhere, in triple-locked and twice-blind files. But not all of the Navy files are gone. Only Logistics. Sclerida doesn't have every card," he concluded with satisfaction. He punched up an action report.

Looking over his shoulder at the dancing holograms, Tira raised an eyebrow. The quality of the images was dreadful and the action was jerky and skittering, people moving about the display as if escaping from a battalion of holographic fleas.

Cousin Helga was wrestling with the end of one of the long, barge-like sofas that had been mangled when Tira's apartments were invaded. Everything began to grow dim in the fading afternoon light. She looked over her shoulder at Tira, sighing. "I wish I could find a better way to do this. But it wouldn't be correct to ask the staff to do it — if there are any left in the building — and it wouldn't be wise to use servobots, because their activities would register on various of the Palace terminals and that might lead to our discovery in a way we would not quite like. Still —" She pushed with all the weight of her slight form against the sofa; it failed to budge.

"We could burn it up," Tira suggested, considering the sofa.

"And the emergency services would come," said Cousin Helga. "And who knows who they would report to, or what they would say."

"A problem," Tira agreed. She stretched and tossed her head.

"If I weren't so tired, I'd think better. Tira, darling; I'm tired, too. I think I'll just pop into my room and try to compose myself," said Helga. Tira nodded distractedly, then slapped her forehead. "What have I been thinking of?" she asked the air and hurried back to Chaney. "Have you tried to tap into the emergency services communications? We might get a better picture of —"

"Who is where," Chaney finished for her. "And it would tell them we're here. You know that locator technique they use, don't you?"

"But if there are a lot of calls, we might have a long time before we have to hide or switch off or . . . whatever we'd have to do," she ended lamely.

"Don't tell me. I realize that they could find us easily, and they would know we've been here. Either they'd think it was looters, in which case they'd lock us in a Security holding cell, or they'd think I'd come back, in which case they'd put us in a Navy holding cell." Her hands slapped against her thighs, sending two small clouds of dust into the air.

"I don't need to say anything. You explain it all very well." He folded his arms as he stared down at the latest display. This one was sharper and steadier than the one before. "I think the Protectorate Office has kicked in. And about time, too."

Tira looked shocked. "The Protectorate? I thought they must have gone to the Navy."

"Not the Protectorate. That's the whole idea. I've been trying to find out what the rest of the Navy is up to," Chaney said. "I haven't got very far. It looks as if the Admiral has been trying to put a lock on everything that might compromise him." The steadiness of his features was belied by the sound of his voice, which was husky with fury.

"Chaney —" she began.

"He is!" he burst out. "He's doing everything he can to protect himself. And that isn't the end of it. He's casting about for those he can suborn. He wants to keep power even if he loses his title and his ships." He took three long uneven breaths. "He's a dangerous man."

Tira made a gesture of sympathy, saying, "It's nothing you can change."

"No, I can't," he muttered angrily. He shoved at the display controls. "From what I can make out, all the rest of the Navy has turned itself over to the Earth Protectorate Office, but the Logistics Garrison continues loyal." He stared at the holograph. "That is the word I want, is it? Loyal?"

"What have they done," asked Tira, unwilling to be forced to defend Admiral Sclerida to defend his son's pride, "in regard to the Protectorate?"

"The Logistics Garrison, do you mean? They've attacked the Protectorate at every opportunity." He flipped through four displays in quick succession: in each of them Logistics Garrison Navy craft were battling with Protectorate ships.

"Oh, dear," said Tira, shocked at the destruction being rained on the Protectorate ships.

"I've found clips and files that show most of the other Navy ships out beyond the space stations. We have about a dozen of the huge Bases on the far side of the moon. For the time being, Naval personnel are being escorted there until there is some resolution to this impasse." He keyed in the codes.

In three-second clips the newest information was displayed on the holograph.

"How can you keep it all straight?" Tira asked as she turned away. "I can't do it the way you do."

"I'm trained for it, and I have a strong left-brain development." There was a hint of amusement in his voice as he spoke and he addressed her with far less deference than he might have the day before. "From what I can tell, the trouble with the military is mostly over. I think the Haiken Maru has lost too much to recover their position, so we shouldn't have to shoot any more Cernians for a while. I don't know what the Kona Tatsu is up to, but I'm beginning to think that maybe all those rumors — the ones we always laughed about? — that they were in charge of the Protectorate, those rumors just might have been right."

"You mean they haven't been trying to stop the Protectorate?" asked Tira in some shock.

"Not that I can discover, no," admitted Chaney with a puzzled frown.

Tira nodded. "You know," she said as a frown line moved up her forehead between her brows, "that could mean Damien Ver is the . . . I don't know what?"

"It makes me wonder," said Chaney. "For the Protectorate to move as quickly as it did to restore order probably means there was help inside the military . . . and since," he went on with greater confidence, "we suspect that the Kona Tatsu has agents in every military service, couldn't it follow that it was Ver who put them into motion when everything was blackest?"

"But why?" Tira asked. "He can't be doing this for love of my step-mother and he knows his birth isn't good enough to advance him any higher than he's risen already."

Chaney nodded, his heart somber. "But together — what if they're in this together? She can't make him High Secretary, but if they were married, it could be that his position would be strong enough for him to gain Senatorial approval to a fait accompli."

"And because he's Kona Tatsu, he might have secrets on the Senators that would strengthen his position? Is that what you mean?" She turned her back on the console where a dozen gunboats were transferring Protectorate officers to the navy craft.

"It's a possibility," he admitted. "I don't know how likely it is."

"Because you don't want to talk about things you might not like?" she challenged. "How well do you think I like them?" Her arms were folded now and her pretty features showed more strength of character than attractiveness. "You're thinking about the need for a diplomatic marriage, aren't you?"

"Well, there are several that could be possible," he hedged, unaware until then at how keen her understanding was. His face felt hot and he was afraid — correctly — that he was blushing. "Your step-mother, of course, and possibly your brother. It could be that —"

"And me. You mustn't forget me." She shoved her hands into the pockets of her work smock. "I haven't forgotten me."

As they talked the holographic display continued to cycle through. It showed two Navy gunboats under heavy attack from a dozen Protectorate skirmishers and a brace of mobile observation platforms. The Navy was being taken in tow by the Protectorate. This gave way to a Marine engineering station where a flotilla of three dreadnoughts with actual ocean-going service ships for support were supervising the change of command from Marine to Protectorate.

"Attention. Priority announcement incoming. Imperial recognition code required," announced the console.

"Imperial recognition code?" Chaney asked.

Tira hesitated, then placed her hand on the genescan plate.

"Word has just reached Protectorate Central Control," said the machine voice, "that Governor Windsor of Harmony Cluster is dead. Repeat: Governor Windsor is dead. We will report as more information is confirmed."

"Governor Windsor is dead," whispered Tira, for the first time beginning to smile with pleasure. "Oh, dear."

"Oh, dear?" Chaney echoed.

"It isn't correct to be pleased by the misfortunes of others, of course, but with Governor Windsor out of the picture, the succession has to go to my brother. I wouldn't mind if it were Jessine. The thing is, it wouldn't be me." She pressed her hands together.

Chaney lost happiness even as she gained it. "Really? It's possible, I suppose." He looked at her. "But They didn't say anything about Anson Merikur. If he is still bringing his forces here to carry out Governor Windsor's policies, what could happen? Either we would have to ratify full and equal status for all members of intelligent species or Windsor's break-away planets continue to sow dissension through the Pact." He scowled.

"I thought you agreed with Governor Windsor," said Tira uncertainly.

"I do. I don't think the Pact has a prayer without granting equality to all intelligent species everywhere. But I think that the Pact needs time to be persuaded to agree. Give immediate rights across the board and there could be a back-lash before the new status quo gets into place; in five years there could be . . . I don't know, guerrillas in the streets, worse turmoil than there is even now."

"That could be difficult," she said, sounding remarkably composed. "But if there was a marriage — finish the rest of it." She swung around and put the console displays on hold. "You think they might reach an agreement with Merikur by arranging a marriage for Jessine or me. That's it, isn't it?"

"I hope it won't happen," he said, revealing much more of his true feelings than he had intended.

"So do I," she said. "Because I won't agree to it. No!" she went on sharply when he made a half-hearted effort to protest. "No. You don't know what it's like, to be told all your life that all you're good for is adding a little oomph to the signatures on documents, that you have to be prepared to be auctioned off to the planet group with the best trade agreements. Well, I do. And I will have no part of it. I am not going to turn into a martyr like my mother, or a manipulator like Jessine, or a nobody flumfluxis like Cousin Helga."

In the last few seconds, the room where they stood seemed to have shrunk. Chaney stared at her, feeling as if he had dived too deeply and running out of air. He forced himself to speak. He could not bring himself to touch her. "What will you do?"

"Whatever I do, it's my business, my business only." She made it very easy for him to kiss her. "The front rooms are terrible," she said a short time later, breathing a little unsteadily herself, "but let me show you the guest room."

"Come," Tira said, leading him by the hand into the guest bedroom beside the entrance corridor. She locked doors between them and the living room, then turned to Chaney.

"But . . . Helga?" he said. He couldn't believe this was happening.

"She'll sleep, I think," Tira said. "Anyway, I left the console on in the living room. I don't think it will distract us."

She began to open the fastenings of her clothing.

"No," he said as he watched her. "Not at all."

Chapter 15

As Wiley continued, he found himself growing faint. He'd completely lost track of time, but he knew he was exhausted and hungry. *And* still feeling the effects of the last party. He found it harder to focus on the direction and speed of the aircar.

"Home," he muttered. "Home is where the . . . is where the food is . . ."

He spotted what he thought must be the Palace landing pad and aimed for it. As he brought the car into a descent, the world unfocused. His head dropped forward.

When he awoke several seconds later, the aircar had crashed to the ground. He turned his head, suddenly too tired to lift it.

He saw a knee by his face, and then he felt the cold barrel of a light-weight pistol pressed at the base of his skull. He remained very still. "Do you mind?" he said tentatively. "That thing's cold."

"My stars!" gasped a voice. "It's Lord Wiley!"

"Milord," said the man kneeling beside him, and withdrew the Meinhauser. "We thought you were dead."

Wiley finally focused on the man's uniform: Secretarial Guard. Wonder of wonders.

"So did I," he said, and started to struggle to his feet.

"Wiley Bouriere," said the corporal in charge of the squad. Awe touched her voice. "We were told all your family were —"

"Dead?" said Wiley and saw the corporal wince.

"It was what we were told," she said. "It was in all the reports."

"Well, they lied," said Wiley. He finally pushed

himself to his feet. "Is there anything to eat around here? I'm starving."

"Yes, there's food, in your apartments," said another Guard, a fair-haired youngster named Garring. "When the assault came and we couldn't reach you, we decided we'd better dig in and wait."

"Even when you were told I died?" Wiley asked.

"Well, we were told, sir, but we hadn't seen . . . well, a body," said the corporal.

Wiley looked at the five Guards surrounding him. They were little older than he was, and unaccustomed to taking the initiative. "Good work," he said. "I'm glad you're here. Now, how about that food?"

The corporal opened her mouth to reply and was cut off by one of her men.

"Look!"

A fully armed destroyer with Logistics flashes was coming in low from the north-east. Its passage stirred up little tornadoes. Aircars in the vicinity were all but knocked out of the air by its turbulence. Laser-cannon and plasma batteries decorated the hull.

It came nearer, blotting out the view of most of the city. The destroyer was a quarter the size of the Palace grounds.

Suddenly all the klaxons, sirens, bells, and whistles of the Palace came to life. The noise was overwhelming.

Wiley crouched down, hands over his ears. He could see the others had done the same.

The noise grew louder as the Navy craft crossed over the Palace wall and continued inexorably forward.

Then someone high in the top of the southwest tower turned a laser-cannon on the Logistics vessel.

Garring was shouting something but Wiley could not hear him over the noise.

A second laser-cannon — this one somewhere on the grounds — opened on the Logistics ship.

The little group on the platform flattened and tried to cling to the surface as huge winds buffeted them, burning.

Wiley tugged at the corporal's sleeve. When she looked up, he gestured toward the nearest entrance. "We'd better get inside," he yelled.

Another blast was fired from the ground station, but the huge ship's shields held against the laser-cannon.

Then another combatant entered the fray, a high-altitude Protectorate surveillance platform. It directed its plasma guns at the destroyer. The platform was designed to bring down armed and

191

shielded spacecraft; a single destroyer was no opposition to its deadly strength.

Wiley tore his gaze from the battle and tugged the corporal's sleeve again. This time she got it, and the group began to crawl toward shelter.

The destroyer was almost on top of them, perhaps seeking to use the Palace for protection, an additional shield to the ones it already possessed.

A missile hissed from the Protectorate platform. But the destroyer's shields held and the mushrooming fire scorched and blackened the upper floors of the Secretarial Palace.

Wiley felt his hair singe and tasted burning at the back of his mouth. He was slightly dazed. His eyes did not focus quite perfectly and he had to resist the urge to simply collapse where he was. *I wonder if I have a concussion?* he thought in some remote part of his brain.

The advance to safety was halted for the moment.

Another missile overshot the destroyer and struck a parking-and-storage building. The spectacular explosion that followed reduced it all to a few broken walls, like a broken child's toy.

A sound, deceptively soft, a deep, crinkling sound as if someone far away had dropped a gigantic chain onto steel, ricocheted along the battered Palace walls.

Then the destroyer, almost directly overhead, shivered a bit, wriggling like a sleeper about to wake. Half a dozen of the turrets came loose and the enormous weapons dangled, two breaking away entirely.

Three lifeboats streaked away from the destroyer, which shook itself again. It drew in on itself, and then opened in a blaze that ballooned upward, suffused with gaudy colors and harlequin patches of black. Twisted metal shapes like lethal party favors began to fall.

Wiley buried his head in his elbow and hoped that if anything landed on him it would kill him quickly.

Ground fire from the hidden lasers brought down two of the lifeboats in blazing wreckage.

But the third lifeboat skittered and bobbed on the ferocious currents of air and miraculously came to rest at the far end of the landing pad. All the lifeboat's guns were trained on the Guards and Wiley.

"There's trouble," warned Garring, speaking loudly against the fading roar of the explosions. "Real trouble."

"Good guess," said Wiley. He looked around. A good part of a cargo hatch, now warped and charred, had fallen from the destroyer and landed not more than twenty paces away. It wasn't the door to inside, but it was better than an open platform.

He nudged the corporal and pointed.

The corporal glanced at the wreckage, then back at the lifeboat. She nodded. "I think we can make it, if we move fast."

"Let's do it," said Wiley, preparing to run.

There were a number of men piling out of the lifeboat, all in Navy Logistics uniforms. They had their weapons at the ready and were forming into three lines.

Wiley and his Guards lit out for the wrecked cargo hatch, finding little purchase on the soot slick surface. They stumbled into the metal just as the Navy troops opened fire.

Hunched down behind the tortured metal, Wiley flinched as another volley of shells left pock-marks in the section of hatch. He glanced at Garring, noticing that the man seemed very calm, taking time to check his ammunition before selecting a place where he could fire.

"There!" shouted one of the Guards, pointing toward the door they were seeking.

Peering around the end of the section of metal, Wiley could just see men in Navy Logistics uniforms piling into the corridor beyond, a number of Cernians with them.

"They have to be Admiral Sclerida's men," said

the corporal. "Who else could get this far? The Protectorate has stopped most of Logistics; these have to be the hold-outs. They couldn't have reached that destroyer without Admiral Sclerida's help."

"We better be ready to fight," said Garring. "We have a sworn duty to uphold." He smiled at Wiley. "Better get flat, sir. In case."

"No," said Wiley. It was one thing for the child he had been to pretend to be a target, with all his personal guards lying on top of him to keep him from getting killed. It was something else now. Death was real now. And enough was enough.

"Better do it now," said the corporal. "Sir."

"Bouriere!" came Admiral Sclerida's voice, magnified by the lifeboat's speakers. "Give yourself up. Come out. Surrender. Or we will open fire."

Wiley stared at the men and women huddled behind the hatch with him. "I can't be a party to this," he said. "I can't let you sacrifice yourselves."

"Sorry, sir," said one of the Guards. "We took our oaths long ago." He smiled a little. "We knew what we might have to do."

"You don't have to get killed," said Wiley in desperation.

"Not unless it protects you," said Garring.

"Surrender, Wiley. You know it's the right thing to do!" Admiral Sclerida urged.

"I don't want you — " Wiley protested to the Guard.

"Better get flat, sir," said the corporal again, ignoring him. "They're about to make a rush from the hallway. And those Cernians look like they're in a bad mood."

"Listen to me!" Wiley ordered through tight teeth.

"When you talk sense, sir," said Garring, and with a diffident shrug, reached forward and shoved Wiley down onto the hard surface of the platform. "You lie real still. You know how to do this. Use that breathing trick." He lay across Wiley, resting on his elbows on the ground and training his weapon on the lifeboat.

The rest of the Guard piled on, each of them taking a position that allowed them to shoot.

Before all the Guard were in position, the Navy Logistics men were firing. The last two Guards on the protective pile were wounded before they could brace themselves.

"Fire at will!" shouted Admiral Sclerida.

Never in the most terrifying nightmares of his youth had Wiley imagined anything as horrendous as this. He lay under a mound of men and women. Bullets, slugs, pellets and beams hammered them, and they shrieked and jerked and shuddered and died, their blood and other things running down, stinking and hot.

He thought he saw Garring's hand, three of the fingers gone and the two remaining with grey matter clinging to them. Wiley was beyond weeping or raging. As his brave Guard were cut to pieces on top of him, he felt their weight on his soul.

Without being aware of it, he lapsed into shock.

Chapter 16

"Which way?" Jessine asked Ver. She was driving now, allowing Ver to concentrate on the communications console.

He had activated the holographic display and was busy searching for new information.

"Take a right, Jessine." He straightened up. "There. I thought so."

"Thought what?" she prompted. She was holding the aircar on course, but having trouble with the sluggish steering. It would take a while to get used to it, she told herself.

"Admiral Sclerida has indeed come out of his cave. Look at that!" He indicated the destroyer drifting in miniature over the display. "He isn't giving up easily, is he?"

"Who isn't?" demanded Jessine as she tried to catch a glimpse of the display while she drove.

"Admiral Sclerida has left his fortress in a newly-accepted destroyer, the *Edward Teach*. He's heading for the Secretarial Palace, I think. He's headed for the city, in any case." He rubbed at the back of his neck, unwilling to admit he was growing tired.

A light flashed on the driver's instruments. "Something coming up behind. Aircar. One," she added as the information was flashed to her. "Protectorate."

"Keep moving," said Ver steadily, working with his console to change the holographic display.

"But if —" she protested.

"Keep moving. I'll take care of things." He was almost ready to bring in a new signal when the speakers of the aircar burst into life.

"Aircar ahead. Aircar ahead. Pull over and hover. Pull over and hover." A Protectorate beacon was flashing on the sides of their pursuer.

"Reduce speed by half," said Ver, and reached over to pull a small concealed lever.

"What's that?" Jessine asked, and then saw on her instrument panel that the Kona Tatsu flashes had been illuminated along with the emergency tabs.

The aircar behind them veered off, putting considerable distance between themselves and Ver's aircar. "Sorry, Kona Tatsu," the speakers said for the retreating Protectorate officers.

"Carry on," Ver said to Jessine as he reached down and secured the lever.

"Very nicely done," said Jessine in approval as she increased their speed once more.

On the display the razed buildings of Haiken Maru Central held Ver's attention as he strove to discover how extensive the damage actually was.

"Another Protectorate aircar coming," said Jessine, and reached for the lever Ver had pulled. She maneuvered the heavy vehicle into a slow glide to permit the Protectorate aircar to read the identification, then resumed her speed and course.

"Very good," Ver told her.

"Thank you," she responded.

"I like the way you do this."

The Haiken Maru ruin vanished from the

display and a new one appeared, one where men in improvised uniforms stormed the Biological Substances Authority, halfway across the city from the Secretarial Palace. Most of them had little more than hand weapons and escape harnesses, but they went at the task with spirited determination, cheering when any one of their number made progress against the formidable bulk of the building.

They went along in silence for several minutes, Jessine concentrating on driving, Ver on the holographs. Then she gathered up her courage and asked, "Damien? You don't have to tell me, but I want to know. I really do want to know."

The tone of her voice alerted him. "Know what?" He watched her closely. "What is it, Jessine?"

"Did you — the Kona Tatsu — kill Cowper?" Her question ended on a gasp, as if she expected anger from him.

His answer was flat. "No."

She took a deep breath. "Do you know who did?"

"Yes." He froze the hologram, suspending a Protectorate squad rounding up a load of truculent Marines. "Kitchley killed the High Secretary."

Jessine stared at him in shock. "What do you mean? Kitchley. That's impossible."

"Keep your eyes on your instruments," he advised. "I'll tell you anything you want to know, but be careful with the aircar." There was real concern in his voice and a sadness in his eyes that was almost as unexpected as his revelation.

She nodded and returned her eyes to the screen and the instruments. "All right," she said, amazed at how calm she sounded. "Why do you say it was Kitchley? He was the most loyal man — Daphnean — on the Palace staff."

"Precisely. But his loyalty was to the Pact, not to the Secretariat, or to Cowper Bouriere. Kitchley was worried about the Pact. He saw the High Secretary in danger, with the Pact slipping more and more into the hands of the Haiken Maru, and Admiral Sclerida trying for a military coup. No matter how many times he was warned, or who warned him, Bouriere refused to see the danger. He refused to take action against Sclerida, claiming it was unwarranted. The High Secretary was convinced it would diminish as time went on, that interfering would only force the issue."

"And it was working, wasn't it?" Jessine asked, her voice a little desperate. She thought of the many occasions when Cowper had promoted that idea — leave well enough alone — to high-ranking visitors and off-planet delegations. He had said he did not want the Pact to look like an oppressor or a conquering army, but a reasonable coalition of dedicated peoples working together.

"No. Kitchley was right. Admiral Sclerida *was* about to launch his coup. That is a fact and we can document it. And he had enough of the Treasury Guard on his side to have let him carry it off." He paused as another update flashed on his console.

The holographic display now showed a skirmisher headed for the Palace. There was a flicker and then a squad of Navy, Marines and Cernians piled out of a huge ground transport at the foot of one of the towers. All were armed and ready for action.

"According to the latest reports, Tira is back at the Palace," said Ver. "Interesting."

"What makes you say that Admiral Sclerida was about to launch a coup?" Jessine demanded.

Ver gave her an amused and distant look; without his affection for her to soften his expression it would have been terrifying. "It's the Kona Tatsu's job to know such things. That's what we do."

Jessine could not argue that. "All right. But I still don't understand why Kitchley would kill Cowper."

"To prevent the coup. Without a major crisis

to disrupt his plans, Admiral Sclerida would have moved to take over within the month. And Kitchley had his own ideas. He was going to hand over power to Admiral Merikur. He thought he could keep the bureaucracy running well enough then. He figured if he did that, he'd have some control over the Secretariat." Ver frowned at the holographic display. "There are still too many armed assault boats in Logistics' hands." He studied the figures running on the display beneath the view of several air fields overflown by Kona Tatsu reconnaissance satellites.

As he watched, a dozen assault boats rose into the air, set in a diamond formation and headed off at high speed.

Ver switched the communications bank on. "Check display feed. What ships are those and where are they going? I want an answer in two minutes. Contact by code." He shut the bank off at once.

"Why not leave it open?" Jessine asked.

"I don't want anyone homing on the signal. Right now only a few Kona Tatsu know where I am. I don't want to change that."

"I just can't believe that Kitchley would do something like . . . like kill the High Secretary."

"You may not believe it, but he did it," said Ver

bluntly. "He had created a strong position for himself in the bureaucracy and did not want to give it up. And he was aware of the dissatisfaction in the client planets. He wanted to change that, and thought that he could, given the chance. He was a patriot — he thought. He thought the bureaucracy could make everything right. He was wrong."

The holographic display suddenly changed and two tiny high-altitude platforms appeared there, engaging each other in heavy fire. The Logistics platform was firing plasma bolts and the Protectorate platform was using laser-cannons. They were carving one another apart.

Jessine glanced at Ver, then back at the controls. "Could the Kona Tatsu take over? Could you have staged a counter-coup against Sclerida?"

He could not see the glitter of her eyes. "Probably, but it would have been very costly."

"And this is an easier way?" She kept her eyes straight ahead. "Marry the widow and you become High Secretary? Is that the plan?"

"Marry the widow is, but not the rest," he said carefully. "I have no wish to be High Secretary. None. I never did." He paused; the two tiny platforms continued to lob destruction at each other. "I wouldn't mind advising one; I'll go that far.

The Pact needs some serious reworking or it will come apart. I don't want to stand by and watch it unravel if I can help stop it."

"Of course," she said in patent disbelief.

"Yes," he insisted with such conviction that she began to believe him. "I am not qualified for the job and I don't want it. But," he added in a gentler voice, "I do want to marry the High Secretary's widow." Before she could think of something to say, he went on. "It wasn't possible before, and I didn't think about it. Now it is possible and it's something I want, if you want me."

Jessine was flustered. "What do you expect me to say?" She mistimed a turn around an abandoned mining building and the aircar rocked as she steadied it.

"I'm trying not to expect anything." He smiled at her. "Think about it, though, will you, Jessine?"

"Ver, this is Command Central. Ships in question are Navy and are under Protectorate supervision. Repeat, under Protectorate supervision. They have been dispatched to the Haiken Maru polar complex."

"Good enough. Thanks," said Ver.

They were over the city at last, and Jessine had to give her full attention to driving. She had the Kona Tatsu identification on once again. Try as she would she could not keep from thinking about everything Ver had said.

"Reports are that there is still fighting at the Palace," Ver informed her as his communications bank came to life again. "That could be a problem if we land inside the walls. We ought to consider —"

"Why did you come after me, then, if you don't want to be High Secretary?" she blurted out, surprising herself almost more than she surprised him.

"Because I love you," he said. "I couldn't bear to see you killed. You are the one thing I'm not willing to lose." With an effort he made himself more professional. "The Kona Tatsu men at Horizon Park were all . . . occupied. I couldn't divert any of them to protect you." He bit his lower lip.

A little later, as they rushed above the chaos of the streets, Jessine said, "I love you too, Damien." As she spoke the words she realized she had never told him before.

"We've got company," Ver said, his holographic display showing three Navy assault boats closing on them from side-streets.

"What do you want me to do?" Jessine asked, all business again.

"Keep going. Make sure the shields are on

full." He coded in for more information but received very little.

The communications bank relayed a message. "Admiral Sclerida has arrived at the Secretarial Palace. The *Edward Teach* makes direct attack inadvisable."

"I should think so," said Ver, giving a critical look to the holographic representation of the formidable destroyer.

"Then what should we do?" Jessine asked, for the Palace was dead ahead of them and they were coming up on the walls fast. "Land? What?"

"Reduce speed," said Ver, and looked toward the windows.

The *Edward Teach* hung over the Palace like a baleful cloud, dark, enormous and threatening.

"This could be difficult," he said to Jessine as the aircar diminished its speed.

From the side-streets the three Navy assault boats appeared, moving quickly to box them in.

Jessine flashed the Kona Tatsu identification but the assault boats did not move off.

"What's this all about?" she asked of the air. "Damien — "

Two short blasts of heavy fire cut across their bow.

"What the — !" Jessine burst out, slowing the aircar still more.

A third shot would have plowed into the nose of their craft but the shielding held while the vehicle bucked and slithered against the impact.

Another shot was fired, this one a hypervelocity missile aimed directly at the power packs.

"It's not responding," Jessine shouted to Ver.

"We're going down," he said, and reached out for her hand.

Chapter 17

Tira was half-dressed as she sat on the end of the rumpled bed. She was reloading her Samtoepoe A7mark923 while Chaney toweled himself dry. "Tell me," she said conversationally, "do you think any of us will make it through this?"

"You mean the coup attempt?" He wrapped

the towel around his waist and began to gather up his scattered clothes.

"Yes. By this time tomorrow, are we going to be dead?" She satisfied herself that the pistol was ready to fire and put it back in her tattered reticule.

"I hope not," said Chaney seriously.

She nodded. "But there's still a chance it could happen, isn't there?"

He was about to dismiss her fears when there was a roaring explosion and the main door of the suite gave way. The sound of breaking glastic and falling debris silenced both of them.

"Surrender! Come out with your hands empty and up!" shouted a rough voice from the entrance to the suite.

Tira had pulled on a loose jacket and was fastening it. She glanced at Chaney and saw that he was tugging on his trousers.

A second burst of fire, which seemed to be intended to demoralize more than harm, racketed through the suite.

"Tira Bouriere! You are to surrender at once!" the rough voice commanded.

Chaney frowned and shook his head. "Keep down," he mouthed to Tira, and moved swiftly toward the door, keeping out of sight.

"If you do not come out, we will open fire again!" the voice informed them.

Tira pulled on her most rugged shoes, hunkering down on the floor to close them.

Chaney gestured to her to move back from her position so that she would have the corner of the armoire for additional protection. He showed his most heartening smile and then inched nearer the door.

"You are ordered to surrender immediately to Admiral Sclerida."

Both Chaney and Tira winced.

They could hear Cousin Helga shriek in dismay.

There was a rush of men in the outer room as they converged on the other bedroom.

"Tira Bouriere, you are officially detained by Admiral Sclerida. If you do not surrender yourself at once we will be forced to open fire." There was bravado in the rough voice now that he had found his quarry.

Chaney scooted backward, keeping low to the floor. As he reached Tira, he said very quietly, "Is Cousin Helga going to be all right in there?"

"The closet is shielded. If she gets inside they'll need more than Kanovskys to get her out. And she knows enough to use the closet." She patted her reticule and the Samtoepoe inside. "This could come in handy."

"My guns are out there," Chaney said unhappily. "I don't think I can reach them."

"Not to worry," said Tira with false insouciance. "There are a few toys in here, under the floor of the armoire. There should be two Meinhausers, and they ought to be loaded."

The noise at Cousin Helga's door redoubled as the Navy soldiers started to use the butts of their guns against it.

"They're heavier than your Samtoepoe," said Chaney in approval as the pounding on the other bedroom door grew louder. "Why doesn't it break?"

"All the interior doors have monocrystalline boron mesh in them. It'll be a while before they knock it down," she said, rummaging at the bottom of the armoire for the release. As she swung back the hidden door, she added, "And there's air packs, too. What do you think?"

"Better safe than sorry," Chaney said, reaching for the breathing unit before he grabbed the Meinhauser. "You better take the other. Save the Samtoepoe for a rainy day." He put his hand to his ears. "Poor Cousin Helga."

"If she's in the closet, she's fine," said Tira as she pulled out the Meinhauser and then the air pack. "We'd better get busy."

"You're right," said Chaney. "We've got one chance for surprise, and after that we're going to need protection. So don't get too far away from this door. Make sure you have cover. And don't try to be heroic. This isn't the time."

"Yes, sir, Lieutenant Chaney, sir." She gave him a mock salute before she slipped on the breathing mask.

He motioned her to keep low, then slid back toward the door. He indicated that Tira should stay behind him and aim for the backs of the Navy soldiers' legs.

"Ready?" he asked.

Tira nodded.

"Here we go." He eased the door open, wide enough to allow him to slide out and provide room enough for Tira to take up a position beside him. He moved smoothly, knowing that the soldiers were more likely to react to an abrupt movement than a graceful one.

He braced himself against the wall and lifted the Meinhauser. He had a clip with sixty rounds and a second with another sixty. That ought to make a dent in the Navy men. He pulled the trigger.

The disruption was dramatic and immediate. Those soldiers who could turned and began firing in Chaney's direction, but more of them fell, yelling with pain as bullets smashed tibias and fibulas and patellas and femurs. The body armor that protected their torsos could not save their legs.

Tira aimed for those who were firing back, deliberately setting about disabling them as quickly as possible.

The floor was growing slick with blood still hot enough to steam.

Chaney swore as a shot grazed his arm.

Several of the Logistics soldiers were already retreating, dragging their injured comrades with them, unwilling to try to fight in such close quarters for so little gain.

"We'll be back!" one of the men shouted as he reached the ruin of the main door. "And you won't get out of here."

Tira, who had been concealed behind the half-open door, made her way around it, next to Chaney, her reticule dangling from her belt, her Meinhauser clutched in her hand. "He means it."

"Yep," said Chaney, trying to find a way to stop his arm bleeding.

"What can we do?" She looked around the room as if hoping for reinforcements. "I guess we could get into the closet with Cousin Helga," she said, thinking aloud.

"We have to realize they're not going to be stupid twice," said Chaney, cursing as the blood ran off his arm and began making a puddle on the floor. "They know this place is hard to crack, and they'll come prepared."

Tira nodded in irritation, then clicked her tongue as she realized how badly he was hurt. "There's tissue cement in the first aid kits in Cousin Helga's room," she said decisively and walked up to the closed door. She bent down and pressed one of the sections of parquetry, clearing the genescan.

The door swung open, revealing Cousin Helga's bedroom. Where Tira's room was rich silkeen and tapestries, Cousin Helga's was all lace and chintz. A plethora of doilies littered every available surface and the two vanity mirrors were held in place by burnished gold cupids.

Helga came bustling out of the closet, a Ridly pistol in her shaking hands. "You can't — " she began, then realized who she was talking to. She dropped the pistol and rushed to Tira's side. "Oh, my dear, thank goodness you're all right. I was so frightened. The noise alone was enough to make one crazed." She looked from Tira to Chaney then back again. "Gracious, what are you doing in those masks?"

"The Logistics men are going to be back," said Chaney. "You can bet on it."

"But surely — " Helga protested, and then her expression changed. "You mean it still isn't over?"

"Not yet," said Tira grimly. "I need the first aid

kit, Cousin Helga. Will you fetch it for me? And bring an air pack for yourself. They might try using gas on us next time, or there could be a fire. Let's get ready to hold them off."

"The double brace still works," said Cousin Helga as she turned to get the first aid kit from the closet. "I didn't have time to put it in place, but we can do it now."

"Good," said Tira, slamming the door closed and coding in the command for the eight steel bars within the door to lock them in. There was a satisfying thunk as the bars slid into place and were anchored. "The first aid kit?"

"Right here," trilled Cousin Helga as she offered it as if it were a tray of sweetmeats. "But I don't see — " And then she caught sight of Chaney's arm. "Oh. Gracious!" The kit slid from her nerveless fingers as she tottered toward her bed, one hand to her brow.

Tira picked up the kit and set to work tending to Chaney's wound. She spoke to Cousin Helga as she worked. "Don't let this bother you," she said, feeling a little queasy herself.

"How did they know where to come?" Cousin Helga wailed.

"I've been thinking about that," said Chaney. "I'm afraid I did it. I think they traced my AID code when I used the communications console.

It's what I'd expect Sclerida to do. It makes sense."

"Yes," said Tira grimly. "It makes sense."

"That means he knows you're here, Tira," Chaney added. He touched Tira's face with his good hand. "I'm sorry."

She did her best to smile. "I know."

"I should have thought —" he began.

There was a sound from the warning beacon near the door.

"They're coming back," said Cousin Helga, reaching for the air pack and putting her mask into place. She gathered up the first aid kit, half a dozen pillows, Tira's discarded reticule, and her antique jewelry box and shoved them all into the closet. "They'll be protected in there," she announced.

Chaney and Tira were already shoving furniture around to increase their protection. The bed was upended and leaned against the door, two of the settees were turned on their sides to provide cover for the three of them.

"It'll take heavy fire to get through the door," said Tira.

"We'd better be ready for it, anyway," said Chaney. "They know what they're up against."

"Not quite. The bars weren't in place before," said Tira, wanting to be more hopeful.

"No. But they may anticipate something of the sort," said Chaney thoughtfully as he set about reloading his Meinhauser. "I would."

"How much warning will we have?" Cousin Helga asked with a quiver in her voice. "I'm not sure I'm up to all this disturbance."

"Who knows?" said Chaney. "I don't think they intend to kill us. Or not Tira, anyway. That's something." He had taken his position behind one of the settees and was trying to find the least uncomfortable position to hold his arm in.

"Do you think they'll use — " She broke off. "Gas."

"That's it," said Chaney, adjusting the flow of oxygen to his mask. "Be careful. Don't take off the goggles, don't rub anything, don't scratch your skin if it itches."

Tira was already rolling down her sleeves and reaching for something to put over her hair. She had been drilled throughout her youth for just such an eventuality and now went about her preparations with rote-learned skills.

Cousin Helga dragged her most elaborate negligee off its hanger and wrapped herself in its vast filmy folds of georgine and lace, all the while whispering imprecations at the attacking troops. "Imagine, storming the private quarters of the High Secretary's family. There's no excuse for it, none."

The gas grew thicker, and even with the masks in place and the oxygen flow on full the rotten-eggs-and-seaweed stench was almost overwhelming. Everything in the bedroom was covered with a fine, acrid mist of unwholesome greyish-green.

"Come out with your hands up. You will not be harmed. Come out with your hands up." This was not the voice they had heard earlier, but a deeper one, more used to command. "Give yourselves up."

"How *dare* they!" fumed Cousin Helga.

"Tira Bouriere. Yon Chaney. Come out." The voice was growing impatient. "If you don't come out, we'll come in and get you."

Tira looked over at Cousin Helga. "Get in the closet," she ordered the old lady. "They don't know you're in here. You heard them. They didn't call your name. Get in the closet."

"But whatever for?" demanded Cousin Helga.

"In case they break through. We need someone who can . . . rescue us, if it comes to that." Tira glanced at Chaney and saw him nod.

"Come out before we open fire. We warn you, we have two laser-cannon trained on that door. We will fire on a count of ten."

Cousin Helga hesitated. "How can I —"

"If you don't hide in the closet, we won't have a chance," said Chaney very seriously.

"One."

"Oh, if you really think . . ." said Cousin Helga, torn between dismay and relief. "I'll be ready."

"Good." Tira all but pushed her through the door, pressing it closed as soon as Cousin Helga pulled the last of her lacy garment inside.

"Two."

"Better get ready," said Chaney.

Tira threw him a kiss before she slipped down behind the smaller settee and swung her Meinhauser up, leveling it at the door.

"Three."

"They'll probably just blow it up," said Chaney. "They don't want to cause too much damage. And they can get in more —"

"Four."

" — easily if there isn't too much damage." He checked his ammunition for the third time, and for the third time swore at how inadequate his supply was.

"Five."

Tira wanted to yell in defiance, to recite the numbers faster so that they would get the fight going. She was tired of waiting. She made sure her goggles were firmly in position.

"Six."

"We're going to get out of this, Tira. We'll be fine," said Chaney, not believing a word of it.

"Seven."

Chaney had a sudden thought — would Admiral Sclerida actually order his death? Would he let his men kill his son? At that moment he would not have liked to wager on it.

"Eight."

"Get on with it," muttered Tira, realizing that the Navy man wanted to irritate her; that recognition made her more irritated than before.

"Nine."

Chaney's hands tightened on his weapon. He prepared to fight.

Ten was announced by a nerve-shattering explosion that shredded the door and sent sections of it flying through the room, smashing the mirrors and wrecking the bed. Chaney's settee was hit by a huge chunk of metal that broke its frame and left one end sagging and shapeless.

No sooner had all the metal landed than a squad of Navy soldiers with Logistics flashes appeared in the doorway, spraying the room with high velocity bullets.

Chaney slipped to the end of the settee and started to pick off the soldiers in the front of the squad, taking care not to waste shots trying to penetrate the body armor protecting their torsos. He aimed instead for the head or the legs, firing steadily and deliberately.

Tira was equally cautious in her shooting, and she succeeded in taking out half a dozen of the Navy soldiers before she became a target and once again retreated behind her settee, prepared to change clips.

There were fifteen men lying in and near the doorway, only two of them still moving. Chaney's next round took out another soldier who landed on top of another dead man.

More high velocity fire kept Chaney and Tira behind their protective settees and played havoc with the decorations of the room.

"You hogmaulers!" Tira shouted, unheard over the gunfire. "We just got this room cleaned up again!" She fired three times and hit two men, one of whom flopped forward, twitching. The other staggered back against his comrades, knocking one of them over as he strove to stay erect.

Then the fire was silenced and the Logistics soldiers moved back from the door.

"Form ranks!" shouted an officer, and the straggling soldiers did their best to comply.

"What in — " Chaney whispered as he watched the soldiers fall back.

In the next instant his question was answered. From the entrance to the suite came a terrible, familiar voice. "Yon. Tira. This is Admiral

Sclerida. I am coming forward. Put down your weapons. My men will not fire on you." The Admiral's footsteps were strangely shuffling and uneven.

Tira remained in her hidden position as a sudden, cold apprehension went over her. She wished she had somewhere to run.

"We are going to work this out," Admiral Sclerida informed them, coming still closer. "You'll see."

And indeed they did, for Admiral Sclerida appeared in the doorway to Cousin Helga's bedroom with Wiley held in front of him as a shield, the muzzle of the Admiral's custom Campriani 56-007 firmly pressed to the young man's temple.

Chapter 18

The aircar jolted into the broken paving with front-crushing force.

"Are you alive?" asked Ver as he unfastened his harness.

"I think so," said Jessine unsteadily. She managed to pry her fingers loose and then unfastened her harness. "Yes, I'm too badly

225

bruised to be dead. I hope you like purple and yellow."

Ver stifled a grin. "On you, my love, any color." He made his way to the hatch and opened it. Another aircar, with Protectorate flashes, was descending.

The other aircar landed and half a dozen Protectorate men hurried out, all with their arms holstered. The man in the lead hurried over to Ver.

"Lieutenant Nkomo, Citizen Ver," he said with a brisk salute and an apologetic air. "Sorry we had to bring you down like this."

"No more than I am," said Ver drily.

"The trouble is," the young man went on, undaunted by Ver's imposing manner, "we have a very bad situation here. It developed very fast, and we're still trying to get solid information on it. You know how hard that can be."

Ver was curious now. "What is the situation, Lieutenant Nkomo?"

"We had to bring you down," said Lieutenant Nkomo, including Jessine in his explanation. "Logistics forces have shot down everything approaching the Palace for the last half hour.

"We have reason to believe that there is a group of Logistics men in the Palace. Our best guess is that Admiral Sclerida is there with them."

"Sounds like a tempting target," said Ver.

"Trouble is, the scanners also show that Tira and Wiley Bouriere are in the Palace as well. They may be hostages." Lieutenant Nkomo scowled. "We've — the Protectorate Office — ringed the entire Palace, but we're not authorized to use heavy weapons against the Palace. We can't put the High Secretary in danger."

"The High Secretary is dead," said Jessine.

"The High Secretary Wiley," Lieutenant Nkomo said. "Sorry, Madame Bouriere."

Jessine nodded. "Poor Wiley," she said.

"I understand," said Ver. "Where is your Situation Command set up, Lieutenant?"

"Not far," said Nkomo. "I can take you there at once."

"Good," said Ver. "Do it."

The Protectorate Office had taken over the Ministry of Horticulture and Agribusiness outside the walls and the Appointments Division inside the Palace.

"Can you get us inside?" Ver asked as he and Jessine got into the Lieutenant's aircar.

"Inside the Palace, sir?" asked Nkomo as the aircar rose.

"Yes." Ver fastened his harness as the aircar banked steeply and shot down the street toward the wide boulevard that would lead to the Ministry of Horticulture and Agribusiness.

"I don't see how, sir," Nkomo answered. "The Admiral's forces —"

Ver reached over and took Jessine's hand. "If I can get inside the walls, all the way to the Palace, do you think you can get me to the Appointments Division?"

Lieutenant Nkomo thought carefully. "I suppose it's possible."

They set down in the central quadrangle of the Ministry of Horticulture and Agribusiness a few minutes later and were at once surrounded by a squad of Protectorate officers in body armor.

As soon as the squad's captain — Harbinger, by his tags — recognized Ver he ordered the men to form an honor guard.

"Lieutenant," said Ver over his shoulder to Nkomo, "please come with us."

The main reception hall had been cleared of its vast collection of potted and tubbed plants. In their places a number of hastily assembled holographic displays were being monitored by Protectorate officers and Kona Tatsu men in black, working, openly for once side by side.

"This is the most recent material we have," said Captain Harbinger, directing Ver to the largest of the displays. "The contact is in Tira Bouriere's suite."

Ver settled down to watch the playback of Admiral Sclerida's arrival.

The figures in the holograph were no larger than rats, and they waited like intangible dolls to be put into motion again.

Jessine found a place near the window, and realized that there were Protectorate marksmen on the roof. She looked toward Lieutenant Nkomo. "You're using snipers?"

For an answer he tried to move her away. "You don't want to make yourself a target. Logistics has marksmen, too." As he spoke, a Logistics man patrolling the balcony on the forty-fourth floor of the Palace lurched and crumpled as a Protectorate marksman found his target.

"Point taken," said Jessine, moving. "How many have you got so far?"

"Thirty-one of them. They've killed nineteen of ours," said Nkomo.

There was a flurry of activity as the holographic console reran the incidents in Tira's apartments.

"How long ago did this happen?" Ver asked as the replay began.

"Four minutes, thirteen seconds," said the Protectorate technician seated at the machine.

Admiral Sclerida appeared, his Campriani clapped to Wiley's head. "We are going to work this out. You'll see."

Tira shrank back, her eyes enormous with horror.

"Let me explain," said Admiral Sclerida at his most genial. "Unless one or the other of you is willing to kill me and — well, High Secretary Wiley Bouriere — you'll have to accept me as the victor. In spite of the set-backs we have encountered, I have prevailed, wouldn't you say?"

No one answered him.

"Well, think it over a short while. It may take some getting used to." He achieved a wolfish smile. "Don't assume I won't kill this boy. I've done worse to get this prize and I won't let him stop me."

"Stop it!" Tira said sharply.

Wiley, who looked very pale and worn, and whose hair and clothes were matted with drying blood, spoke up. "Don't give in. It's all for nothing if you do."

Admiral Sclerida tightened his grip on the boy. "Shut up."

"Don't listen to him," Wiley said.

"Wiley!" Tira cried out.

"Does it bother you, Tira, seeing him like this? I found him under a pile of dead and dying Guards. It seemed they were trying to save him." His chuckle was unbearable. "I kept him from being crushed. Didn't I?"

Wiley did not answer.

"So, for you and" — he smiled again — "for all those watching this, here are my terms. You are to recognize me as the official guardian of the late High Secretary's two minor children, that is, Tira and Wiley here, and give me full discretionary powers in all Pact matters. Or you can kill all of us and the Pact will go into chaos. One or the other. Your choice."

Ver stood back from the console. "Four minutes ago, you say?"

"Closer to eight now," said the console technician.

Jessine stood behind Ver, her hand to her mouth. "Stop him. Stop him."

Chapter 19

Chaney was proud to have Tira beside him as he faced his father across the littered floor. His Meinhauser was pointed toward the floor but he held onto it with determination.

The Navy soldiers had been ordered back to the door, and they gathered there now, staring in at the confrontation.

"You'd better kill me," said Wiley quietly. "You can stop him if you kill me. He won't have anything to —"

"No," said Tira.

"No," Chaney agreed. "That isn't the answer."

"It's for the Pact," protested Wiley. "If he gets his hands on it, he'll run it into the ground."

Admiral Sclerida laughed. "I had no idea you cared so much for the Pact."

"Neither did I," said Wiley quietly. "But I won't let it fall to you."

"Then your sister will have to kill you. Or my son will have to kill me. And then, naturally, my men would be forced to open fire. So you see, you really have no choice." The Admiral was very pleased with himself and smug in his triumph.

Tira half-raised her weapon, then faltered.

"Of course, you, Tira, could shoot me and Yon could shoot your brother. It might be easier that way." Admiral Sclerida beamed at Chaney. "Do you think she'll do it, son?"

"Don't call me that," said Chaney.

"If I am — shall we call it regent? Yes, let's. If I am regent, then you will advance very high in the world. You will not have to be a lieutenant any more. You can command whole battalions, for all I care, and become a Commodore before I die."

"I'm not interested," said Chaney.

"Why don't you kill us, then?" asked Tira. "Get it over with?"

"First, because I am enjoying myself. Second, I happen to need you. You are pawns, but very necessary pawns. Once I am established, that will be another situation, and it may be that you will hamper me. But both of you are young and well-born, and should be worth something at the bargaining table. No doubt I can use one of you to sweeten a truce with a marriage?" He laughed again, and spoke to Chaney. "That would bother you, wouldn't it, Yon?"

"If you're trying to goad me into shooting you, you're doing a good job," said Chaney tightly.

Admiral Sclerida saw the anger in his son's eyes. "I think it would be a good idea for you to put your gun down now. You're getting over the shock of seeing me. Put it down. Or I will injure this boy very badly." This time there was merry anticipation in his smile. "Or shoot me."

Chaney ground his teeth. His arm rose once and he tried to aim the Meinhauser at Admiral Sclerida. But he could not force himself to shoot his father, and he damned himself for his weakness. The pistol slid from his fingers and clattered to the floor.

"That was sensible of you," approved Admiral Sclerida. "You don't believe it now, but in time you'll see you've done the right thing."

Half-turning to Tira, Chaney whispered, "I'm sorry."

"It's all right," she said, and raised her own gun.

"Ah, ah, ah," warned Admiral Sclerida, the aim of his Campriani shifting from Wiley to Chaney. "He may not be able to shoot me, but I have no such hesitation to kill him. Put your gun down, or you can watch both of these men die."

Reluctantly, Tira shifted her grip on the pistol to the end of the butt and let it down easily to the floor. "Don't hurt either of them."

"Not if it isn't necessary," said Admiral Sclerida. He made a dismissing gesture. He signaled his remaining troops. There were only nine of them still alive and unwounded, and they responded to his summons with alacrity, their weapons up and ready.

"We must make arrangements for you. Now that you are orphans, it is the least that I can do." He released Wiley, pushing him away. "Go to your sister. And you, son, come here."

"I don't think so," said Chaney as he drew Wiley between him and Tira.

What Admiral Sclerida might have answered to this defiance none of them ever learned. Like Nemesis herself, Cousin Helga burst out of the closet, Tira's Samtoepoe A7mark923 clutched in her hands like a two-handed sword of God.

"You *killed* him. He was a *saint* and you *murdered* him!" she shrieked as she cut the Admiral and his men in half with the intensity of her firing. "You will not be *permitted* to *live!*"

Her fingers were still locked around the trigger when Tira at last pried the empty gun out of her hands.

Epilogue

The recently restored Grand Reception Hall of the Secretarial Palace was filled to capacity with representatives from throughout the Pact. The activities had begun a week before with the inauguration of Yon and Tira Bouriere-Chaney as joint High Secretaries. This afternoon had seen the ratification of the new terms of the Pact alliance. Tonight's gala was — almost — purely social.

"I'm glad you're the one taking the job," Wiley admitted to his sister as they wandered through the crowd. "I know I don't have the temperament to handle it." He looked older now than he had just three months ago; there was a graveness about him he had lacked before.

They smiled as the one surviving Daphnean of Rainbow Dawn approached. Hanley, a former under Appointments Clerk, supported himself with a cane and there was a welt of half-healed scar across his forehead. He nodded to Tira. "Good evening," he said. "It is splendid to see everyone here tonight." He nodded at the medley of beings surrounding them. "This week has been a promising beginning. I hope that we can continue this way."

"With the devotion shown by those of Rainbow Dawn, I'm sure we can," responded Tira.

Hanley smiled. "Thank you, Madame."

"Are you sure you won't reconsider staying on Earth?" asked Tira. "Truly, your experience and insights would be most valuable to us. To the Pact."

Hanley shook his head. "Thank you, Madame, but I think it's time I retired. I look forward to sitting in my garden with my grandchildren.

With you and your husband in the Palace, I feel safe in leaving such matters in younger hands."

Tira blushed a little. "Thank you, sir. I hope that your grandchildren will enjoy your company, for they are depriving us."

"You are most gracious." Hanley gave a half-bow and another smile, then turned away. Someone had called his name. "Good evening, Madame, Sir."

Damien Ver approached as Hanley disappeared into the crowd.

Tira smiled at him and found herself wondering how she could ever have thought him cold and uncaring. "How are you managing in this mob?"

"The same as I have for the last week," he replied. "I review the holographic tapes at the end of the day and check the delegates' registry to make sure I know who's who." His smile was quick and amused. "Have you seen my wife anywhere in the last half hour?"

"She's talking with the Peomer delegation, over by the beverage table. They seem to believe that because she is now Advisor to the High Secretaries, she must be courted." Tira linked arms with her brother and . . . what was he? Her stepfather-in-law? Her friend.

Wiley could not enter into the amusement. "I

don't envy any of you," he said with feeling. "You have decisions to make that I could never —"

Ver cut him short. "You have other decisions you're willing to make. Undertaking to be the Pact's Inspector-General is quite a job in itself. You know that some of those old-fashioned leaders aren't going to give up their hegemony without a struggle. If you want to keep the Pact honest, you're going to tangle with some real villains. I'll back you all the way, but I don't want your job."

A small band was set up in an alcove and it was blaring away with *Pact Victorious* followed by *Glorious Heritage*. In that part of the Reception Hall the din of conversation was at shouting level to be heard over the band.

"Cleaning up after the Haiken Maru is going to be the beginning," said Wiley with the first show of enthusiasm. "Once that's settled, then we can show real reforms. There are so many obligations we have left unfulfilled."

"But you don't have to do it all yourself," said Tira, trying to ease the burden her brother had taken on.

"Yes," he countered her. "Yes, I do. I owe it to Nika and all those dying Cernians and my own Guards, every one of them. I will never forget any of them. They died to keep me alive, and I have to merit that. I don't now, but maybe in time, I will, a little." He smiled tentatively. "At least this way I'll have a chance."

Tira relented and laid her hand over her brother's. "If you must, you must."

Wiley gave Ver a slightly embarrassed look, then broke away from his sister. "I'll join you for the ceremony, but I want to talk to Anson Merikur." He moved away, threading through the bustling crowd with surprising speed.

"What do you think?" Ver asked of Tira when a few seconds had gone. "Do you think he's going to do it?"

"Whatever it is?" Tira said. "Yes, I think he will. But who would have thought that Wiley would be the one to devote his life to the service of Pact justice?"

"It doesn't seem all that far-fetched to me," Ver remarked, then leaned toward her. "And I notice that Chaney is on the balcony watching us."

Tira looked up at once, and grinned at Chaney as their eyes met. "It's almost time."

They started toward the dais. Tira rubbed absentmindedly at the two thin scars on the back of her hand, left by shattered glastic.

"Only two weeks, and everything changed," she mused.

"For the better, let us hope," said Ver. He exchanged polite greetings with Anson Merikur's second in command and was pleased to see that Lieutenant Nkomo was with him.

"We're counting on you and Jessine to make sure of that," said Tira. "The non-human council begins its congress next week. Everything we've assessed this week is supposed to be used then. It hardly sounds like much, but it's a start."

"Never forget that it is only a start," Ver advised, and then his expression changed as Jessine, in a glorious confection of sea-green silkeen with gold beading came through the crowd toward him, leaving the Peomers to devour the last of the scallop steaks, eyes fixed on Ver.

Watching the silent exchange, Tira said to Ver, "Please, tell me Chaney and I are not as bad as you two."

"The style is different," Ver said, "but the content is the same."

At that Tira laughed aloud and attracted the attention of a great many of the huge gathering. She was about to dismiss their interest when she decided that this might be the best time, better than the formal ceremonies planned for the conclusion of the evening banquet. This was the right time to call them all together, she decided, and so she made her way to the dais, motioning to her husband and brother to join her there. Ver took Jessine's hand and joined them.

"Members of the Pact," she said, and waited while the band fell silent and conversation faded to a faint buzz. "Members of the Pact, we are about to begin a new phase in our community of peoples. For the first time the promise of the Pact will be a promise given to all member-species of reason."

Tira's family was gathered around her now, and the delegates flocked toward them.

"We have all seen the terrible cost we pay for inequality in the Pact. No one who values the Pact can wish to see this continue. Therefore, after long thought and the advice of countless human and non-human Pact members, we are inaugurating a writ of equality applicable to all sentient species within the Pact. From this day forward, all sentient species will enjoy equal status and equal rights, with all the protections and responsibilities accruing thereto."

Now Chaney was beside her. "We have pledged," he said, taking up her thoughts, "to enforce laws uniformly throughout the Pact, and have taken it as a mandate to reform the exploitations and hardships which have existed previously. For there will be equality within the Pact or there will be no Pact at all."

243

The cheer began raggedly but grew until the Reception Hall rang with it, and it faded slowly, leaving an expectant hush behind.

"There will be other crises, and other dangers, ones that we cannot anticipate now," said Tira, pausing to make sure she had the full attention of every delegate in the Reception Hall. "But this I promise you. We all promise you. The danger of inequality will never be tolerated again, so long as the Pact endures."

Chaney held up his right hand. "The Pact!" he called out as if leading the entire glittering crowd into battle. He took his wife's right hand.

"The Pact!" she echoed with deep emotion.

Wiley laid his right hand above theirs. "The Pact!" he declared with a fervor that would have moved their father had he heard it.

Jessine and Ver offered their hands as well, with the same victorious cry.

Gradually the delegates pressed forward, reaching to add their hands to the knot, shouting again and again as if with one voice "The Pact! The Pact! The Pact!"

GRAND ADVENTURE
IN GAME-BASED UNIVERSES

With these exciting novels set
in bestselling game universes,
Baen brings you synchronicity at its
best. We believe that familiarity with
either the novel or the game will
intensify enjoyment of the other.
All novels are the only authorized
fiction based on these games and
are published by permission.

THE BARD'S TALE™
Join the Dark Elf Naitachal and his apprentices in
bardic magic as they explore the mysteries of the
world of The Bard's Tale.

Castle of Deception
by Mercedes Lackey & Josepha Sherman
72125-9 * 320 pages * $5.99   _____
Fortress of Frost and Fire
by Mercedes Lackey & Ru Emerson
72162-3 * 304 pages * $5.99   _____
Prison of Souls
by Mercedes Lackey & Mark Shepherd
72193-3 * 352 pages * $5.99   _____

And watch for **Gates of Chaos** by Josepha Sherman
coming in May 1994!

Paksenarrion, a simple sheepfarmer's daughter, yearns for a life of adventure and glory, such as the heroes in songs and story. At age seventeen she runs away from home to join a mercenary company, and begins her epic life . . .

ELIZABETH MOON

THE DEED OF PAKSENARRION

"This is the first work of high heroic fantasy I've seen, that has taken the work of Tolkien, assimilated it totally and deeply and absolutely, and produced something altogether new and yet incontestably based on the master. . . . This is the real thing. Worldbuilding in the grand tradition, background thought out to the last detail, by someone who knows absolutely whereof she speaks. . . . Her military knowledge is impressive, her picture of life in a mercenary company most convincing."—**Judith Tarr**

About the author: Elizabeth Moon joined the U.S. Marine Corps in 1968 and completed both Officers Candidate School and Basic School, reaching the rank of 1st Lieutenant during active duty. Her background in military training and discipline imbue The Deed of Paksenarrion with a gritty realism that is all too rare in most current fantasy.

"I thoroughly enjoyed *Deed of Paksenarrion*. A most engrossing highly readable work."
—Anne McCaffrey

"For once the promises are borne out. *Sheepfarmer's Daughter* is an advance in realism. . . . I can only say that I eagerly await whatever Elizabeth Moon chooses to write next."
—Taras Wolansky, *Lan's Lantern*

*　　　*　　　*　　　*　　　*

Volume One: Sheepfarmer's Daughter—Paks is trained as a mercenary, blooded, and introduced to the life of a soldier . . . and to the followers of Gird, the soldier's god.

Volume Two: Divided Allegiance—Paks leaves the Duke's company to follow the path of Gird alone—and on her lonely quests encounters the other sentient races of her world.

Volume Three: Oath of Gold—Paks the warrior must learn to live with Paks the human. She undertakes a holy quest for a lost elven prince that brings the gods' wrath down on her and tests her very limits.

*　　　*　　　*　　　*　　　*

These books are available at your local bookstore, or you can fill out the coupon and return it to Baen Books, at the address below.

POUL ANDERSON

Poul Anderson is one of the most honored authors of our time. He has won seven Hugo Awards, three Nebula Awards, and the Gandalf Award for Achievement in Fantasy, among others. His most popular series include the Polesotechnic League/Terran Empire tales and the Time Patrol series. Here are fine books by Poul Anderson available through Baen Books:

THE GAME OF EMPIRE

A *new* novel in Anderson's Polesotechnic League/Terran Empire series! Diana Crowfeather, daughter of Dominic Flandry, proves well capable of following in his adventurous footsteps.

FIRE TIME

Once every thousand years the Deathstar orbits close enough to burn the surface of the planet Ishtar. This is known as the Fire Time, and it is then that the barbarians flee the scorched lands, bringing havoc to the civilized South.

AFTER DOOMSDAY

Earth has been destroyed, and the handful of surviving humans must discover which of three alien races is guilty before it's too late.

THE BROKEN SWORD

It is a time when Christos is new to the land, and the Elder Gods and the Elven Folk still hold sway. In 11th-century Scandinavia Christianity is beginning to replace the old religion, but the Old Gods still have power, and men are still oppressed by the folk of the Faerie. "Pure gold!"—Anthony Boucher.

THE DEVIL'S GAME

Seven people gather on a remote island, each competing for a share in a tax-free fortune. The "contest" is ostensibly sponsored by an eccentric billionaire—but the rich man is in league with an alien masquerading as a demon . . . or is it the other way around?

THE ENEMY STARS

Includes for the first time the sequel to "The Enemy Stars"; "The Ways of Love." Fast-paced adventure science fiction from a master.

SEVEN CONQUESTS

Seven brilliant tales examine the many ways human beings— most dangerous and violent of all species—react under the stress of conflict and high technology.

STRANGERS FROM EARTH

Classic Anderson: A stranded alien spends his life masquerading as a human, hoping to contact his own world. He succeeds, but the result is a bigger problem than before . . . What if our reality is a fiction? Nothing more than a book written by a very powerful Author? Two philosophers stumble on the truth and try to puzzle out the Ending . . .

CHANGE THE FUTURE!

All you have to do is read the two endings for *Podkayne of Mars*, the one as originally published, and the one as originally *written* by Robert A. Heinlein, and decide for yourself which is the better ending. Then send us your vote.

Whichever ending gets the most votes will be published as the one true ending in all future Baen editions of *Podkayne of Mars*. (Robert A. Heinlein's defense of his original ending will be published in future editions of *Podkayne of Mars* as well!)

$1,000 CONTEST

Baen will also be awarding prizes for the best short essay defending your choice of endings. *Five hundred dollars* goes to the grand prize winner, and fifty dollars to the ten best runners-up, and *every* person who votes will receive a free *Podkayne of Mars* full-color poster. Deadline for entries is January 31, 1994.

For entry blank and details see *Podkayne of Mars*, 0-671-72179-8, $10.00.